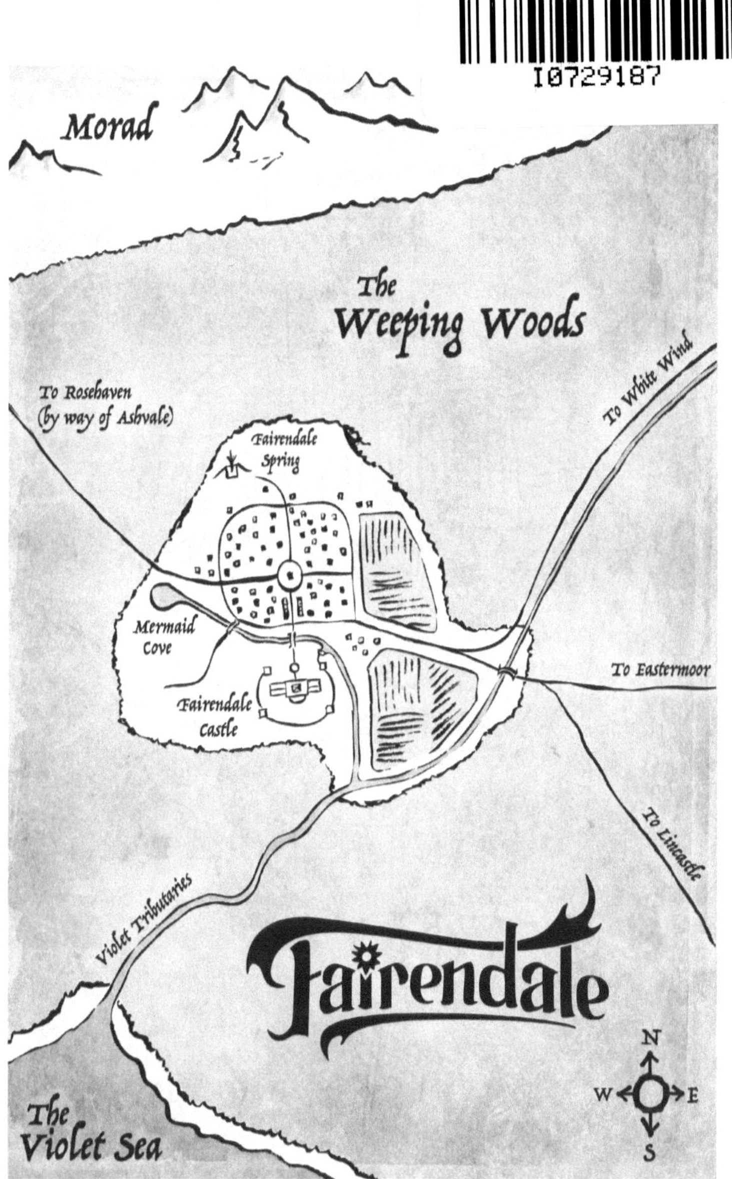

Morad
The Weeping Woods
To Rosehaven
(by way of Ashvale)
To White Wind
Fairendale Spring
Mermaid Cove
Fairendale Castle
To Eastermoor
To Lincastle
Violet Tributaries
Fairendale
The Violet Sea
N
W
E
S

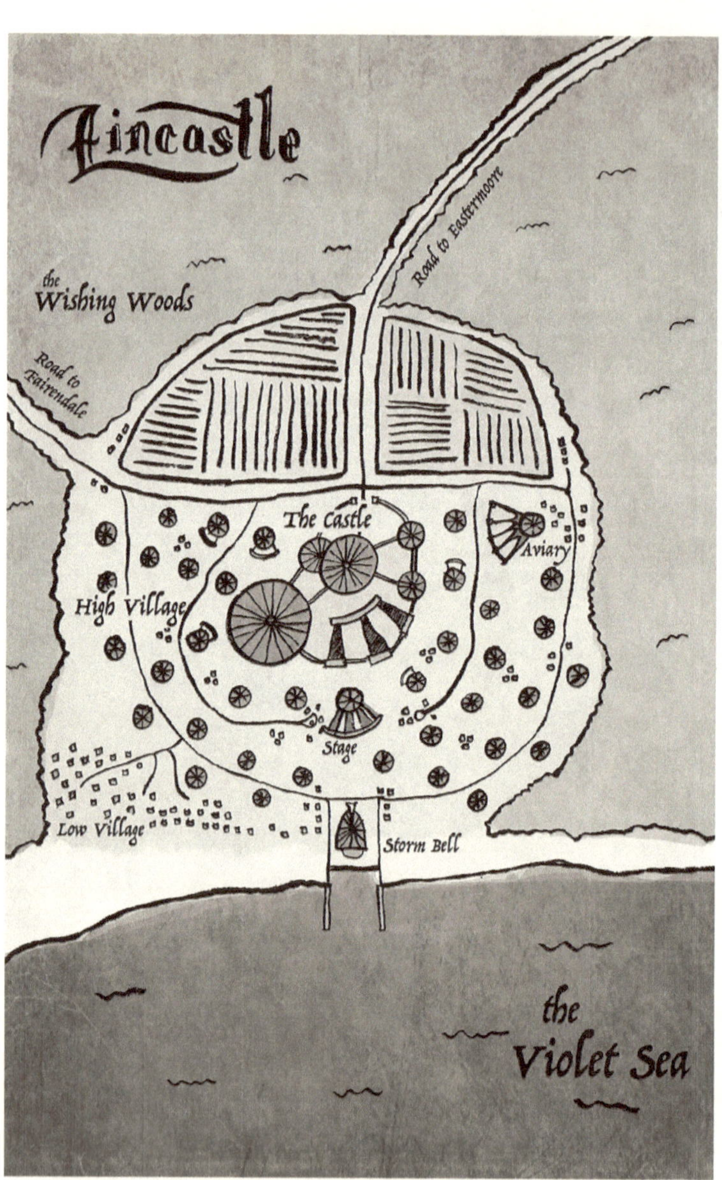

Aincastle
Road to Eastermoore
the Wishing Woods
Road to Fairendale
The Castle
Aviary
High Village
Stage
Low Village
Storm Bell
the Violet Sea

Fairendale

13

THE
WOMAN WHO
STOLE THE THRONE

Read all the books in the Fairendale series!

Book .5: *The Good King's Fall (a prequel novella)*
Book 1: *The Treacherous Secret*
Book 2: *The King's Pursuit*
Book 3: *The Perilous Crossing*
Book 4: *The Dragons of Morad*
Book 5: *The Fiery Aftermath*
Book 6: *The Mysterious Separation*
Book 7: *The Boy Who Spun Gold*
Book 8: *The Boy Who Robbed the Rich*
Book 9: *The Girl Who Awakened the Beast*
Book 10: *The Boy Who Became the Wolf*
Book 11: *The Girl Who Built the Tower*
Book 12: *The Boy Who Loved a Swan*

Collector's Editions:

Books 1-6: *The Flight of the Magical Children*

To see all the books L.R. Patton has written, please click or visit the link below:

www.lrpatton.com/writing

L.R. PATTON

THE WOMAN WHO STOLE THE THRONE

BATLEE
PRESS

Published by
Batlee Press
Post Office Box 591596
San Antonio, TX 78259

The author appreciates your taking the time to read her work. Please consider leaving a review wherever you bought it and telling your friends how much you enjoyed it. Both of those help get the book into the hands of new readers, which is incredibly important for authors. Thank you for your support.
www.lrpatton.com

Names: Patton, L.R., author.
Title: The woman who stole the throne / L.R. Patton
Description: First edition. | Batlee Press, Texas:
Batlee Press Books, 2019

10 9 8 7 6 5 4 3 2 1

First Edition—2019

Illusions

It is a mostly brilliant day. The sun is reaching long golden fingers toward the browning land of Fairendale, though clouds gather in the sky, hinting that the sun will not be out for long. It never is anymore. Cook lifts her face to the sky and breathes. She will take what she can, for however long she can. She has missed the warmth.

Cook, who is more than a mere cook at Fairendale castle and functions as a household manager of sorts, is today walking the perimeter of Fairendale castle, which is large and sprawling and, for this task, requires practically an hour. She admittedly walks slowly, purposefully, doing something that no one within the castle would guess she is doing—except, perhaps, the boy called Calvin, who is her assistant and who watches her every move, particularly now that she has returned after a lengthy absence. The king's page, Garth, might also guess; he and Calvin have, after all, witnessed her shape shifting ability. Or so she suspects. She has seen them whispering behind cupped palms in the hours since her return.

Cook possesses the gift of magic, so it is, perhaps, opportune that most of the castle staff have fled in the days since the king's roundup, a militaristic strategy wherein he commanded his guards to seize all the children of Fairendale and, instead, caused a catastrophe so sizable as to chase away castle staff, the village children, and the entire king's guard (she hopes, that is, that the men who served in the king's guard have been merely chased away and not destroyed by the dragons of Morad, as the rumors suggested).

It is a long and complicated story, but suffice it to say that King Willis regrets his actions of the past, and in the coming days, he would like to make reparations for them.

So he says.

Cook has heard him say this; she is not sure she believes him entirely.

Around the perimeter of the castle Cook ambles, one strong and steady foot in front of another. As she walks, she touches the walls of the castle, and if one were looking closely, or if one had the gift of magical sight, one might see a spark of green flash from her fingers, roll over the walls, and become a wall itself. A second wall. An invisible wall that only those with the gift of detecting magic can properly see. She reinforces this magical wall around the stone walls of Fairendale castle in the same meticulous way she earlier reinforced one on the border between the castle grounds and the Weeping Woods.

Cook is not only the cook and castle manager; she is also the castle guardian. Her magic keeps monsters out.

Currently, Cook is unaware that there is already a monster who has breached her protective wall. She was gone for a good many days, and it has been some time since she has attempted this spell; it is likely that the lag time between her departure and her return left just the right amount of space for a monster to slip through. She will know soon enough. And the guilt will eat at her.

Before she left Fairendale castle to secure a magical spinning wheel in her shape shifter form—a bear—Cook performed this same ritual every early morning, from the time she first arrived at the castle as only a lowly cook's assistant. She would secure the border around the woods and walk the perimeter of the castle and touch its walls and repeat the ancient words, after which she would take a brief nap, to revive herself from the magic expenditure. Only then would she prepare breakfast for the castle staff and the royal family.

She plans to do the same today. It is good to get back to ritual and routine. She has missed it.

The protective spell she put on the castle the last time she was here included an extension. It was a somewhat elementary one, to be sure, but one that tended to last longer than most, without need of frequent reapplication. She did not mean to be gone so long. Cook looks at the walls. She hopes it was effective. If not, today's will be. She wills her magic into the stone walls, her hand trailing beside her.

Though the castle is emptier than it has ever been, the people within it deserve the highest protection.

But before Cook can complete her circular walk around the castle—when she is almost to the castle steps in a complete revolution—a voice startles her. "My Lady!"

Cook looks up. It is Calvin, her assistant. He has never called her "My Lady," and this confuses Cook. Her eyes bore into his. He seems to realize his error, but his face registers confusion, as though he is not quite sure what to call her. Is it because he witnessed her shape shift? Did he see the form she used to have, the young royal princess that always returned in the moments before her preferred form (that of a castle cook)? Did she mistakenly let the image linger? She cannot remember. It could very well be so.

Cook presses her lips together and says, "I am only a castle cook, Calvin."

"Yes, My Lady," Calvin says. His eyes meet hers and flick to the ground. "I mean, ma'am."

"I suppose you have interrupted me for good reason?" She does not say what she was doing; he is an observant boy, so he will likely already know. It is not wise to speak about it, at any rate. He will know this.

Cook does not like to see the boy so flustered. She was, to be quite honest, surprised by how happy she felt to see Calvin again. In her years working with him, though he is far from a good cook and more often than not is a hazard to have in the kitchen, she has grown fond of him.

"Yes, ma'am," Calvin says at last.

Cook waits for him to tell her the reason he has interrupted her, but he bites his lip instead. She extends her hand and touches the castle wall, another bit of green magic sparkling. Calvin's eyes widen.

So he is gifted with the ability to see magic. Well, it was only a matter of time before he discovered her secret.

"And what is it you have come to tell me?" Cook prompts him.

The boy straightens his back, as though he has

suddenly remembered what he wanted to say. His eyes grow even wider, if possible, and he says in a breathless voice, "It is a monster."

Cook cocks her head. "A monster? What is this you say, boy?" Fear vibrates in her chest, but she tells herself to calm, to wait, to listen.

"A monster, in the castle throne room." The boy's voice is squeaky and unsure.

A monster in the castle throne room? Cook's heart thumps harder. "A monster has breached these walls?" Cook stares at her hands and then at the walls of the castle. Either her magic is not working or the protective spell she used in her absence did not hold up. She hopes it is the latter, though it would not surprise her if her magic is waning; she has never spent so much time in her bear skin as she did on this last quest. Magic needs maintenance. Practice. Stretching.

Her shoulders sag, but for the boy's sake, she tries to straighten them again. No sense in letting him see her defeat. Cook looks at the boy, whose fear she can nearly taste.

"Is it a dangerous monster?" she says. It is a silly question. Every monster is dangerous, is it not?

But Calvin says, "I do not know. She looks like a… person?" The words lift like a question.

"A person who is a monster?" Cook is more confused than ever.

"Like the walking dead," Calvin says, and Cook shivers. But at least it is not one of the terrifying creatures. She can work with the walking dead. They do not move fast enough.

Cook nods once, dismissing Calvin, but he remains on the castle steps.

"I will be with you shortly," she says. She must ensure that her spell is working now. They cannot have more breaches. She must close the gaps. She looks at her hands and calls up the magic. The green spark remains. She must still possess the gift. It must have been her absence, then.

"What would you have me do?" Calvin's words startle her.

Cook eyes him. She says, "Stay in the kitchen. Monsters never go into the kitchen."

Who knows if it is true? It does not really matter, does it? She will be finished momentarily, and then she will search for the monster.

The walking dead. It has been some time since she has encountered one of those creatures.

Calvin nods his head and flees.

Cook stares at her hands again. They are young

hands, but she is not so young. She is still strong, though, and she continues weaving her spell, fortifying the walls, protecting those within. She closes the remaining gaps by touching the brass knocker, a bear, that hangs on the front of Fairendale castle's heavy oak entrance. The brass bear glows green—a brilliant, flaming version of the color—and roars.

It is finished.

Cook enters the castle, the musty smell of the monster leading her straight to the throne room.

Yasmin reclines her blue-hued body on the Fairendale throne. The throne is rather large, and she is thin and wiry, so there is plenty of extra space around the contours of her body. She folds a leg underneath her rump. When that is not sufficient, she stretches out her legs, both of them in front of her. When that is still not sufficient (the cold gold is uncomfortable; perhaps she will have the padding replaced), she sighs and stands.

The king has not returned to this throne room since she frightened him away, but that is perfectly fine with her. She has plans for him. She will execute them in time. For now, she is enjoying the feel of this throne (well, not exactly enjoying; reveling, perhaps, at her newfound power?) beneath her. She sits again and places her arms across the golden curves. Her shoulders feel as though they are even with her ears.

She is not a small woman, but this throne makes her feel small.

It was not made for a woman, and this reality annoys her to no end. A woman can rule a throne as well as any man, and Yasmin aims to show the world how wrong it has been.

The whispering begins as soon as she sits and ends as soon as she stands. She does not have much use for the whispering; she is a woman of her own command (well, mostly), and what the throne whispers is of no consequence to her. She can see, however, how it might have helped a man like King Willis, a man of indecision. She smiles, supremely satisfied with her strong will and determination. The throne has told her all the destruction she will bring to the realm, but it has no idea what she plans.

Yasmin taps her fingers on the gold. Does she really want to be bound to a throne? It is true that Fairendale is a rich land, the land that rules all the others, but she suspects that in her former life, she never desired a throne. The desire is nowhere to be found, even now, as she searches the depths of herself.

But she was given a directive by someone: by whom? She remembers speaking words into a mirror: "We shall have the kingdom we always deserved." Who is we? Yasmin and…?

She thinks it might have been the Grim Reaper; she was once linked to him, was she not? But now, in the warm and flickering torchlight of Fairendale castle's throne room, she has lost the connection.

No matter. She will have to reestablish the connection (maybe), which she likely can do by traipsing through the woods (does she really want to?). She is not afraid of the creatures (or is she?); she is their leader (does she want to be their leader?). They would never hurt her (or would they?).

Yasmin presses both hands to the sides of her head. Her thoughts move in circles, tormenting her with questions and doubts.

She is just about to head toward the throne room doors so she can escape into the woods, consult her master, when a thought stops her: Does she not enjoy being in charge of her own actions, unswayed by what another wants?

She drops into the throne again.

Yes. She does. But the problem is that she does not

have a plan of her own. Everything that has unfolded in her mind is the gift of the Grim Reaper. She is, after all, only a woman who has been raised from the dead. Without the Grim Reaper, she is…

Nothing.

Yasmin swallows hard and shoves herself up out of the throne and strides in what could be called a graceful, elegant manner toward the mirror positioned off to the side of the ornate wooden platform on which the throne sits. She gazes into the glass. She does not look like a monster; she believes she is quite beautiful. She touches her blue-tinted cheek (the smooth one, not the stitched one) and blinks her long-lashed eyes. They are dark pools of life. She is alive, even if not quite.

The thought both soothes and alarms her.

A small gash—or wound, or something; she does not know exactly what happened—on her right cheek has been stitched up, large black threads poking through skin. As soon as she finds the right kind of Healer, she will heal this facial monstrosity.

Something clatters at a window. There are many in this throne room, lined up against one wall that faces the village of Fairendale. But it does not take Yasmin long to see what has made the noise.

It is only a shadow, but she can tell it is a bird.

Yasmin cocks her head. A bird, come to visit her? Why?

She moves toward the window, holding her breath, silencing her feet. Birds are sensitive creatures that detect the smallest of shifts in movement, but this one is different. This one does not move, as though it does not see or hear or feel her coming. She picks up her pace.

In truth, Yasmin has the ability to move faster than is humanly possible, a gift of being both alive and dead at the same time. She reaches the blackbird, which is about one hundred feet across the room, in a breath, and she has plucked a feather from its body before the blackbird can lift into the sky and fly away to safety.

It does not bother to fly at all, in fact.

Yasmin grins at the feather and lifts her chin. She turns back to the blackbird, which meets her gaze with its beady black eyes. "I know what you are," Yasmin says. "I know why you are here."

And she does, now that she has held a feather.

Someone is spying.

Yasmin swipes the bird with a vicious flick of her wrist, and the blackbird falls from the windowsill, down, down, down to the ground. It does not move when it reaches the grass, and Yasmin laughs a hollow laugh.

She turns from the window. If the bird is still on the

ground later, she will use it for one of her potions. But, for now, she has a feather. She looks at the feather, delight lifting her spirits. She traces her cheek with its soft quill. It was so easy, plucking this feather, taking what was not hers. She hardly even feels bad about it.

Her old self, what remained of it, is falling away.

The quill pulses in her hand. Yasmin stares at it. Magic? Can there be magic in this quill? She has not felt magic in so long she wonders if she is mistaken. But there it is again: the electrical charge that jolts her fingers and shakes through her body.

Magic. She will possess magic again, with this feather.

Her laugh rings out into the silence.

Lovely.

She attempts to use the quill like a staff, but nothing happens. She tries again. And again. Nothing happens, but the electric charge grows brighter, more intense. She pinches her lips together, clenches her jaw, and squints her eyes. The quill has magic, but it is useless.

A thought occurs to her. She writes *broiled salmon* into the air, with invisible ink, and a plate clatters to the ground. On it is a slab of pink salmon, black pepper dotting it.

Yasmin's eyes widen. She writes *steamed broccoli* into the air, and the plate once again appears. This time she is ready for it; she catches it and sets it beside the salmon. She writes, *Lemon meringue pie* and there it is in front of her, a whole pie, the white meringue browned at the top, just the way she likes it. She can eat the whole thing.

Her fortune has taken a decidedly positive turn.

Yasmin looks around the throne room—at the elaborate paintings of giants and battles and kings and celestial skies on the ceiling; at the torches flickering along the walls; at the ruby red carpet that stretches from the throne room entrance to the platform that elevates the throne. It will be lovely to rule this throne for a time. She will enjoy every minute.

But first, she will eat.

Outside the castle, beneath the throne room windows, the blackbird remains on the ground. He does not move for some time. And then, unexpectedly, he does. He flutters one wing followed by the other. He attempts to peel himself from the ground, but he cannot manage yet. He has been stunned not only by the fall but by the magic ripped from his body. The monster has stolen something important, and the bird is none too happy. He twitters angrily on the ground, careful to do it quietly so the monster will not hear and return for—what?

Feathers. The monster stole one of his feathers.

Shadows gather. The blackbird watches them shifting and swallowing. He will be missed soon. He must get up.

The blackbird wills himself to stand and fly back to the village of Fairendale, where a fire and a hot meal awaits him inside a cottage. And, at last, with all the strength he possesses, he rises. He flies. He returns.

The home to which he flies is the home of a village woman with flaming red hair: Cora. Only, before he walks into this small cottage (where there is, alas, no fire), he is no longer a blackbird but a sleek black cat.

Cora has been so absorbed in her thoughts and plans —thoughts and plans that have no logical order to them but resemble a chaotic mass of tangles—that she has neglected to build her evening fire. There was a time, a short period of time, when she did not have to bother with the fire. Sir Greyson, former captain of the king's guard—and former sweetheart of Cora until he chose allegiance to the king over allegiance to her (she is still angry with him)—ensured that it was done every evening.

Since their falling out, Cora has been tending the fire herself.

She does not mind. She is a self-sufficient woman, capable of caring for herself. She was capable of caring for her daughter, too, before Mercy disappeared when the king's men—Sir Greyson leading them; how could she have forgotten?—invaded the streets of Fairendale and captured some children in cages and sent the rest fleeing for their lives.

Cora rubs her burning chest. She hopes Mercy is as capable of caring for herself as Cora taught her to be. There are important tasks to be done before Cora turns her attention to searching for her daughter.

The guilt throbs in her throat. She shoves it away.

She bends to touch the bandage on her leg. She cleaned away the blood and stopped its flow with a bit of thick cloth as soon as she returned from the dragon lands, which is where she picked up the wound. Her dragon— she is a rider now, though it is the last thing in the world she expected or wanted to be—nipped her with his teeth before she had fully shifted into her blackbird skin and darted away. She had not even known such a thing was possible—a dragon wounding his rider. She hopes he feels it, too. The wound is much deeper than she had originally thought, and it is remarkably painful. It will take some time to heal.

Cora's black cat, Grimm, weaves in and out of her legs, as though trying to comfort her, as though saying all of this will work out the way she has planned, as though proclaiming there is nothing to fear. But Cora knows there is plenty to fear. She has never been more uncertain about her place in the unfolding of fate; mere days ago she had thought she was meant to lead the people of Fairendale in a revolt. But then she became a dragon rider. And then she lost her magic.

The people no longer trust her. They trust Sir Greyson and his liquid lies more than they trust her.

(No, that is unfair to Sir Greyson; he is no liar. He has never had need to lie, and perhaps he has never told one in his entire life. She would not be surprised. He is perfect, which is why it would never have worked out for them.)

The thought that pulses in Cora's head, right above her eyes, is one that means drastic change and an embrace of the unknown. Perhaps even the dangerous. It is this one: Count your losses and move on.

Move on where? It is not yet clear.

Cora blows out a breath and pats Grimm on the head. "Hello, Grimm," she says. "I am glad you returned. I was looking for you for some time."

This is not entirely true; she only called for him a time or two at her door. But she is exceedingly glad for his company right now.

Grimm licks her hand, his sandpapery tongue catching on her skin. Cora notices a bald patch on his belly. "What happened to you? Did you fight a monster?" Cora laughs at herself. She runs her hand along the spot. Grimm meows. Cora looks into his green eyes dotted with flecks of earth, and she laughs again. "I bet you won."

As she intends to do.

Cora rises. She will not bother with a fire this evening. It is already too late. She will curl up in her bed and sleep. Which is precisely what she does.

If she had remained awake, however, she might have seen Grimm flash into a man—a very old man with wrinkles carving rivulets on his forehead and down his cheeks and beneath his bottom lip. A man with eyes so blue they seem to be plucked directly from the summer sky at noon. A man with a decidedly strong body, still, in spite of the testaments of age that mark him.

The man flashes so swiftly from cat to man to cat again that it is enough to make one wonder if one's eyes are playing tricks.

It is enough to make one wonder if eyes can be

trusted at all.

The cat curls up next to Cora's side, black tail wrapped around his body, tip resting on the bare patch of skin.

Decisions

Matilda was wandering out in the woods of White Wind, trying to gather what herbs she needed to heal the latest sickness of one of the villagers (there had been so many she could hardly keep them straight), when she heard something that might indicate the presence of another person. A silent something that may have only been her imagination.

But Matilda's mother had warned her, many times, about the dangers of showing magic in her homeland. And Matilda held in her hands a staff—one made of rich, white, gleaming wood. Of course it could be dismissed as a walking stick (a rather fancy one), as most magical people's staffs could be dismissed, but the problem was that Matilda had not once let the staff's bottom end touch the forest floor as she walked. If someone were spying and paying close attention, they would know she did not need it for walking.

In the historical books of White Wind were stories of sorceresses who had once been burned at the stake. The people of White Wind were distrustful of those with magic, because of a long and troubled past.

Magic, Matilda knew, was nothing to fear. She should not be ashamed of having the gift. But she was not a foolish young woman. She ducked behind a tree and reduced her staff to a layered pearl necklace that circled her neck three times.

Three was a good number, her mother had always said. A lucky one. As though luck had anything to do with magic.

But Matilda pressed her beads into her neck. She closed her eyes.

The person to whom the silent steps belonged was an old prophet, one she had never seen before. At least he wore the black-gray robes of a prophet. They flapped about his ankles. His white beard hung down his chest in a knotted tangle. His hair, of the same color and disarray, was long and stringy, matching both his eyebrows and the fluff above his mouth.

If not for his gray-black robe, he would look like a cloud walking.

He did not look around, and Matilda thought that perhaps he had not seen her. She remained behind the tree, pressing herself flat, holding herself still, until he said, "Come out, my child."

She was no child. In fact, she had a child of her own, sleeping in a sling on her chest.

Surely he was not talking to her.

"I am a prophet, my dear," he said. "You cannot hide from me."

Of course. Prophets know everything.

So Matilda emerged. The prophet wore a pale, wrinkled face that was touched with pink at the cheeks. It was the kind of face that knows laughter and pleasure and joy. One can always tell.

Matilda felt instantly drawn to him.

He had strange eyes—yellow around the edges, dark green in the center. She had never seen eyes quite like them before. They made him look much younger than he had, at first, appeared.

The prophet bowed low. "Matilda," he said when he had risen.

"I am sorry," she said. "I do not know who you are."

The prophet smiled, and the wrinkles around his mouth and eyes deepened. She knew she was correct to assume he was jolly. "I am Bregdon." And what followed was a tangle of names that Matilda knew, instinctively, added up to his full name. The one prophets kept secret, because it granted control to those who possessed it. They could be Summoned, used, enslaved with that name.

Matilda was shocked by the trust he placed in her.

Bregdon. He had been a prophet of White Wind. He had not been seen in some time.

She did not get a chance to ask him about this; he approached her swiftly. "I need you to make something for me," he said.

"What would you have me make?" Matilda said. Apprehension gurgled in her throat. She kissed the top of her baby's head. He would not ask her to make something dangerous, with a baby strapped to her chest.

"A magical spinning wheel," Bregdon said.

"I can no more make a magical spinning wheel than you can." Matilda glanced at her arms, marked with the decorative flourishes characteristic of Healers, and stared at him, hoping he could not see the magic in her.

But, of course, he was a prophet.

"But you can," Bregdon said. "And you will."

She felt slightly annoyed at this proclamation. Matilda was the sort of person who liked having a choice, which is why she did not much like prophets, always proclaiming the future. She preferred changing the future. Prophets had learned to stay away from her.

This man, however, had not known her long enough to steer clear.

If she did not have the baby strapped to her chest, she would fold her arms across it.

Instead, she turned away.

"Please," Bregdon said. There was a note of panic in his voice. Well, good. She was her own woman; she would never do what a man told her simply because a man told her to do it. "Hear me out, my dear."

"My dear," at least, was better than "my child." And there was a difference in his tone. It was not the tone she had heard from men all her life: the one that said they were entitled to whatever gifts she had, which she had been given for their purposes. His tone was that of a desperate prophet, one in dire need.

So Matilda turned back around.

"This spinning wheel will be able to accomplish much in the realm," Bregdon said.

Matilda had read of the great works of Bregdon the prophet. He had given a significant number of prophecies in his long life (she could not remember how long that life had been). All of them had come true. It was highly unusual for every prophecy a prophet foretold to come true; some of them prophesied for their own gain or to bring about events that they themselves wanted to see happen in the realm. Some of them were simply daft, stringing together words for the sake of an audience.

Bregdon, however, was known—or had been known, rather—far and wide for his accurate prophecies. Sometimes he brought good news, and sometimes he brought bad. But he always, it seemed, told the truth.

"What have you seen?" Matilda said. She had never been a prophetess, and she had always desired the Sight. But she had been reunited with her magic, though she was a mother, and it was supposedly, according to her own mother, better to be a second-time sorceress, if the magic chose to remain in her. Which it had.

"I have seen a great many things," Bregdon said. "But, alas, they are not mine to share yet."

Matilda looked at Bregdon for a very long time. She fixed on him her steady gaze, the one that told swindlers and those who sought personal gain that she was not to be trifled with. This gaze made most of them crumble. Bregdon stood strong, and it was she who relented.

She knew only of this prophet through stories, but there was something about him, something plain and open on his face, besides the mirth lines, that told her she could trust him implicitly. It would be difficult, later, to explain why. But her heart had never led her astray.

First, however, Matilda would stage her false resistance, test him for his true nature. She kissed her baby's head again and straightened.

"I cannot do magic anymore," she said. She gestured to her infant. "I am a mother." She held out her arms. Though her skin was a deep brown, the lines marking it could be seen, swirls and spirals and flourishes twisting and turning over every inch of her forearms. The lines decorated every part of her but her face. "Healing is all I can do now." It is all she had ever claimed to do in White Wind.

"I know who you are," Bregdon said. "I know what you can do."

She did not feel afraid, as she might have if the words had come from any other person. Bregdon was no danger. She knew this. She could feel it.

"You have a strong gift of magic," Bregdon said. "And I need it."

"For your own purposes?" Matilda said.

Bregdon shook his head. "Never." And with that one word, the force with which it was said, the passion and power and sincerity balled up within it, Matilda knew.

She knew she would make the spinning wheel.

"Will I do harm by creating it?" She could tell that

Bregdon knew, by her words, what she had chosen, too.

Bregdon did not answer, only smiled.

"For what will it be used?" she said.

"Many things," Bregdon said. "Turning straw into gold, administering sleeping spells, spinning thread and yarn, as it was originally made to do."

She supposed she could overlook the fact that he had not answered her question about harm. After all, who could know the whole future? Could not everything be used for harm, when in the wrong hands?

At least this is what she told herself.

She created the spinning wheel, with a strong magical spell covering it, and Bregdon promised to hide it until the proper time it was needed for use. She wondered at this "proper time" but did not ask. Perhaps it was better not to know everything; she could not be implicated if she did not know. Bregdon disappeared in a cloud of wispy white smoke, as though he had never been there at all, as though nothing out of the ordinary had transpired inside the White Woods of White Wind.

In Matilda's hands were the herbs for which she had been searching. She smiled. She was rather tired; he must have known.

She turned back toward the village and headed home.

Uncertainties

It is a frightening sight that unfolds around Maude, mother of twin sorcerers Hazel and Theo and wife of Arthur, the former instructor of magical studies in the village of Fairendale. She stands in the middle of a clearing inside the Weeping Woods, between two houses that were cloaked in invisibility before the Enchantress— or whomever successfully executed the Vanishing spell responsible for carrying all the fleeing Fairendale children away to their new homes and their new identities— completed the plan for the children's escape. The children were fleeing the pursuit of King Willis, who sought to eradicate a magical child he thought threatened the throne of Fairendale.

Maude allows these remembrances to flip through her mind; it is better than concentrating on what is before her.

What is before her is a scene straight from one of the horror histories Theo enjoyed reading in their village home, before magic upset everything they knew.

Maude, poor soul, is surrounded by figures clad in black robes. They have the blackest and most bottomless eyes the world has ever seen. The few times Maude has looked up, into their faces, she has felt as though she is slipping into death, into the underworld, into nonexistence. The monsters—or whatever they are—all wear a similar mark on their right eye, though each has its own shape. The marks look as though someone took a quill pen and drew feathers or spider webs or simply ornate flourishes on the cheek and forehead and temple near the right eye. Their skin is so white it is almost blue.

They are much too close to her, but at least they are no longer moving closer.

Though Maude has tried her best to ignore him, there is one at their center more terrifying than the others. His face is covered by the black hood of his robe. He carries a scythe.

Maude knows who he is. She trembles.

After all this time, after everything she has survived—the slashing swords of the king's men in the streets of her village, the journey through the creature-filled forest, the encounter with dangerous dragons—she will die here, near the shoe-shaped house with her apron full of fresh vegetables. Well, no longer full; she dropped them in fright, only moments ago.

Maude shakes her head.

The Grim Reaper walks slowly, purposefully, toward her, his scythe above his head. Maude cringes and trembles more every step he takes. The black-eyed people are not moving, however, and she turns a circle just to make sure. They remain where they are, as though they are waiting for a sign from their leader. What will happen when he gives them that sign? Will they consume her? Will it hurt?

Maude wishes Arthur were here. He would know what to do. He was always better at thinking on his feet. She has no magic left; she does not see a way out.

"What do you want with me?" Maude's voice is tight and strangled, her throat nearly completely closed to air.

The Grim Reaper lowers his scythe and folds down his hood. His face is ghastly, like the face of a skeleton peering through stony skin. He has no eyebrows or eyelashes, only the deep black pits for eyes and a mouth with teeth sharpened to a point, fixed in a terrifying grin. He twists his scythe and lifts a bony finger.

She cannot hear what he says, but she can read his

lips. "You," he whispers, and the wind begins to howl.

Maude wishes she had been content with the food she found in the Enchantress's pantry. She wishes she had not been so determined to have fresh vegetables in the soup she was cooking—which is still cooking in the house she can see from here, the house where her daughter sleeps, hanging between death and life. A pain scratches at her chest, insistent.

Arthur would likely call her foolish for doing what she did. And now Hazel will be all alone in the house of the Enchantress, with a boiling pot of soup that will surely burn more than the room it is in.

Maude glances toward the house. It is much too far away. If she could only run, if she could reach it, if she could hide behind its protective spell…

Is there a protective spell? She certainly hopes so. Once the Grim Reaper is done with her, she does not want him to destroy her daughter.

Does she want the fire to destroy Hazel? Which would be the most merciful end?

The Grim Reaper seems to be enjoying her discomfort. He stands for a while longer, grinning at her, pointing his stony finger, while Maude's mind sorts through more questions: What does it mean to be taken by the Grim Reaper? She knows it will mean death, but what kind of death? Is it the sort of death that requires walking the earth like one of these…monsters?

There are no stories to help her. She supposes no one has ever survived an encounter with the Grim Reaper.

Maude feels sick.

She wishes she had a chance to say goodbye to the ones she loves.

Arthur.

Theo.

Hazel.

She will not know if Hazel ever wakes from her sleep. She will not know if Theo survived his flight from the village of Fairendale. She will not hear the stories Arthur will tell of his time with the dragons—she is, of course, sure he is still alive. Arthur could survive practically anything.

She will not know what became of the lost children of Fairendale.

Maude brushes away a tear.

And perhaps that is what the Grim Reaper awaited; he begins to move now, closer and closer and closer. Maude swallows hard. She can almost smell his rotted breath, can almost feel his sickening, icy-cold touch. He lifts his scythe again, his eyes gleaming, and Maude closes her eyes. So she will die, then. What else had she expected?

"I love you," she whispers, hoping the words will carry across all the distances between her and Arthur and Hazel and Theo. Perhaps her sacrifice will keep the Grim Reaper away from all of them. She can only hope.

Maude lifts her chin and raises her arms at her sides. She will die courageously.

It takes a very long time for the Grim Reaper to do what he is going to do. In fact, it takes him so long that Maude opens her eyes again, and, to her surprise, the Grim Reaper and all the monsters in his army have vanished.

There is only empty space between her and the home of the Enchantress.

Maude does not ask any questions. She knows well enough what to do from here: she runs, as fast as her legs will carry her, back to the home where Hazel sleeps.

But before she reaches the steps of the cottage, Maude, in a rare moment of overwhelming fear and relief and exhaustion, collapses, her head coming to rest gently against the green carpet of the Enchantress's yard.

An old woman—a very old woman, judging by the bend of her back—emerges from the line of trees and gathers Maude in her arms, with more strength than one might expect, and carries her into the cottage, where she lays Maude in the bed beside her daughter.

The Grim Reaper feels the haze of confusion settle over his whirling mind. He is in another part of the Weeping Woods, along with his people. He is no longer in a clearing at all; the trees grow much too thick here to be called a clearing of any kind. What has happened? He turns around, looking for the woman—the woman with magic. Where is she? What has she done?

As the knowing settles over him—the knowing that he has lost yet another magical person—the Grim Reaper releases a noise so deafening that the entire woods shake. He is growing weary of this game that he cannot seem to win. He flickers in and out of visibility. He must conserve his energy; it will not do to dwell on his losses. He knows he will need to remain strong for what he has planned ahead. His body, his slowly solidifying spirit, was not ready. It seems that the woman could see him, but he could not yet touch her. He must grow strong enough to touch them, to gather souls at will, and then he will be unstoppable.

There will be more opportunities. He is sure of it.

It is only a matter of time.

The Grim Reaper raises his scythe in the air and brings it smashing to the ground, where it vibrates against the earth. He and his people vanish in a cloud of gray smoke.

"Where is he?" Mirth, one of the three Graces of Fairendale—a watcher of the realm, protector of the seven kingdoms—peers into a magical looking ball. It is the time of evening when she and her two sisters check in on the lands and their people.

They had seen the Grim Reader and his army gathered inside the Weeping Woods near Fairendale. They had seen the woman in danger. They had almost intervened—but someone else had done so first.

An old woman. A sorceress. Who is she?

They do not know.

Good Cheer shakes her head. "I believe he has cloaked himself in invisibility," she says. "He must have known we would be watching. He does not want us to track him." She pauses, wriggles her fingers. The looking ball does not shift but continues showing the clearing and the shoe-shaped house and the smaller cottage with flowers ringing it. Good Cheer tilts her head, studying the looking ball, as though trying to figure out what it is saying.

Is the Grim Reaper still in the clearing? Does he still pose an immediate danger?

Good Cheer says, "He will not always remain invisible to us. It requires too much magic, and he is trying to conserve his."

"For what?" Splendor says. Her red hair curls around her shoulders, a flame to the charred green of her dress. Only golden sequins tell of her origins: Splendor was once a queen.

"To take the people," Good Cheer says. "Without death requiring it."

The sisters, who were not always sisters but who have become such through their shared service to the realm, stare into the ball, each one as puzzled as the other. How is it possible for the Grim Reaper to take where death is not already present?

"It will be some time before he is strong enough," Good Cheer says. The knowing is deep within her.

"But he grows stronger every day," Splendor says.

"So we must keep our eyes on him," Good Cheer says.

"But he is invisible," Mirth says.

"Not for long," Good Cheer says. "He is not

permitted. The Graces must know everything that is happening in the realm." Every sunrise, every birth of a child, every death of a man or woman, every animal's prowl, every sinister plot, every giant's war. They must know it all.

It is the way of the realm. It is how it has been since they became Graces.

Still, Good Cheer's voice does not sound entirely convincing. And all their hearts tremble around the words, *What if?*

"So you have come to Fairendale castle." A voice rises around Yasmin. "For what?"

She has only just finished eating the supper she summoned for herself, none of which, she was disappointed to note, she could taste. Her chest feels tight and heavy, and a dull ache throbs behind her eyes. The last thing she wants right now is company.

Yasmin looks toward the doors in front of her and skims over the windows and glances behind her, where another door leads into the dining hall. She did not use the dining hall this eve. She did not want to be seen.

No one is here.

And then she sees the mirror, a faint blue glow emanating from its frame. Someone stands inside the mirror. A king. She knows this king, recognizes him, though he was not a king when she knew him. She squints her eyes. She is not mistaken, no. He was hardly a man when she died, but she would know those eyes anywhere. The man in the mirror is Sebastien, her son. She feels nothing—no pride, no joy, no love—at this fleeting observation.

"Who are you?" the man in the mirror says, as though he can see into her mind.

She certainly will not tell him.

Instead, she stands and walks nearer to the mirror. She places a hand on its oval edge, which is lined with golden and turquoise flourishes tangled around one another.

It is strange, this vision. Sebastien—he must be a king; he wears a crown—paces, but there is no room behind him, so it looks as though he is walking on air or on nothing at all. Yasmin tilts her head and touches the mirror. The glass ripples, but it does not give.

Yasmin walks behind the mirror, examining its wooden back, and when she finds nothing to explain the illusion, she moves back to its front, where King Sebastien is waiting, a sour look upon his face.

"Where are you?" Yasmin says.

"You did not answer my question," King Sebastien says. She can see, by the way his eyes flash, that he does not know where he is. Does he know how to escape from wherever he is?

He was her son once, but she knows nothing of what happened after she left the world as his mother and woke again as Yasmin. How did he become a king? Did he die? Is he preserved in a mirror? Before she can ask any questions, he says, "What do you want with Fairendale?"

This is not an easy question to answer. She is not entirely sure what she wants with Fairendale. She only knows she was urged to come here, to the flagship of all the lands. But for what?

She has not yet connected with the Grim Reaper since coming to Fairendale castle. He will be angry with her, and the thought makes her shudder.

Tonight. She will connect with him tonight. In the woods beyond the castle.

King Sebastien's eyes narrow. "Do I know you?" he says. "Have we met before?"

He cannot possibly know her. She is too changed now. Death dismantled her, and the scientist, the man who calls himself the Prophet Iddo, put her back together and gave her a new opportunity at life. She tries not to hold it against him. Magic would have been much more powerful and effective for the task than science, but perhaps he used what he had. That is all anyone can ask, is it not?

The former king, trapped in a mirror, has grown impatient. He puts his hands on his hips. "I will ask you one more time," he says. "Why have you come to Fairendale?"

"If I do not answer, you will do…what?" Yasmin arranges her face into the most innocent expression she can manage. She is having great fun with this man in the mirror, this former son. She must have loved him once. But now, well. They are beyond the bonds of love.

What she does not tell this man is that if she knew why she had come to Fairendale, she likely would not tell him. He is in the mirror for a reason, perhaps to protect the land, perhaps to preserve himself, perhaps for another reason altogether. It makes no difference. Her plans are her plans (or, rather, the Grim Reaper's), and they are no business of a former king trapped in a mirror.

King Sebastien glares at her through the looking glass. "You dare defy a king?"

She does not remind him that he no longer holds the throne because he is kept within a mirror. She simply says, "Why are you in there?" She looks at him steadily, curiously, boldly, to prove that she is not the least bit afraid of him. She is, after all, his mother, though that life is far removed from this one.

He looks at her without blinking. His lips are nearly white, so pressed are they. His eyes are thin slits. His arms form a wide, flat X in the middle of his chest. But then his chin lowers and his shoulders hunch, if only slightly.

"The mirror sustains me," he says in a voice that is much smaller and much thicker than it was before. He stares at the ground for a long time, enough time for Yasmin to feel the blow to her chest, the tingle of her skin, the cold breath that whips down her back.

So he *is* dead. And alive, too. Like her.

His next words are like another stone colliding with her chest. "And what sustains you?"

So he knows.

Since he has been so forthcoming with her, she decides to return the favor. She says, "Science. Necromancy, perhaps. A blend of both."

"You do not know what keeps you alive, what keeps you in the world?" King Sebastien's words come out between clenched teeth, and Yasmin tilts her head. Is he angry with her for this not knowing? And how can he blame her? She was dead and then she was alive. She never asked for any of it.

"I was created by someone in a secret laboratory," she says.

King Sebastien's eyes widen now, but Yasmin pretends she does not see it. It would not do to make this man in the mirror afraid of her, not when they might help each other out of their suspended states. Not when she might use him to reveal the mysterious secrets of this castle. Not when he is her son.

She strikes this last thought from her mind. She is attached to nothing and no one.

Yasmin reaches for another question. "Why are you kept alive?"

"It was my own doing," King Sebastien says. "Many years ago—a way to preserve myself."

"How?" she says, but she can tell that he does not want to say, not yet. No matter. She will win his confidence in time.

"And you?" He turns the question on her.

"I had no say." The words are out before Yasmin can stop them. She would like to take them back, but they dangle between them both, peering at one and then the other, raising more questions.

"You did not want to live again?" King Sebastien asks the predictable. His arms drop to his side, his back straightens, and his eyebrows lower. It is his way of showing disbelief, she remembers.

Did she want to live again? She has no memory of her old life, beyond the knowing that this man was her son and that she must have loved him. She does not even remember her old name. Was it a good life? Was she satisfied to have lived it? Had she asked for immortality, whatever the cost?

She does not think she would have. But she does not answer the question. It would be unwise.

After a time, once King Sebastien likely realizes Yasmin has no intention of confirming his suspicions (she can tell they are his suspicions, because his face is as readable as the sky), he says, "Who are you?"

"I am called Yasmin," she says. No sense in trying to recall her old name; he would not believe her even if she could. And though he has not asked it of her again, she says, "Perhaps I have come to restore the realm." It sounds as though it could be true. The words root in her chest, unfold, and begin to grow.

Restore the realm. The possibility vibrates through her.

King Sebastien's eyes fix on her. The smile that turns up his lips is unreadable. In his eyes is a look of such intense hunger that Yasmin feels a line of cold dew drip down her spine. "Perhaps we might help one another, then."

A memory grips her shoulders. A smile, when he was young and innocent and full of promise. It is not the smile of this man before her. She shakes her head to clear away the memory. She is not that woman anymore. She is a husk of who she once was. She is Yasmin, the walking dead, raised to life by science and electricity.

The former king beckons her closer, but Yasmin remains far enough away so that if he reached out from the mirror, if he could, he would not touch her. She is not afraid of him, no. She is more powerful than a man in the mirror. But there is something about him, something broken, something that could, perhaps, be fixed by the right person.

Is she the right person?

She dares not hope. A person—a creature—such as her is not made to repair what has been broken; she is made to break what has been restored.

King Sebastien lowers his voice. "There is a pile of bones in the dungeons beneath the dungeons," he says. "They belong to me."

"Why are your bones in the dungeons?" Yasmin says.

"All you need to know is that if my bones are returned to the throne, they will come alive again." King Sebastien folds his arms across his chest. "I will be released from the mirror. I will live again."

Yasmin studies him, the self-assured tilt of his chin, the eyes that watch her, the mouth still turned up. He has no doubt that he will live again.

"You must return my bones to the throne," King Sebastien says. "It has restorative properties. It is an apex of dark magic." His words have an authoritative tone, and Yasmin can see that while he may not have been a good king, he had been a proficient one.

She does not answer. Her heart pulls her one way—her son could live again—and another—but then there would be a powerful king on the throne of Fairendale. She tries to listen for the voice of the Grim Reaper. She hears nothing.

King Sebastien continues to stare at her expectantly. So she says, "Once I have finished gathering my army of creatures, I will free your bones." She has some time. And ambiguity buys her more; after all, will she ever be done gathering her army of creatures? She has not yet been directed to even begin, so it could be weeks, months, years.

King Sebastien is not happy with this answer, however. His eyes grow dark, and another cold line of dew drops down Yasmin's back. Her heart feels as though it will fly apart. He is her son. He is not her son. He is evil. He is misunderstood.

Which is it?

"You must get them now," King Sebastien says in a voice as cold as the air in Guardia's underground caves.

Yasmin stares at him for a moment. She tries to find the boy she once knew, the boy she once loved, the boy who once loved his mother. When she cannot, she turns away.

"Yasmin!" he calls. She does not look back. She walks toward the throne room doors, farther and farther away from the magic mirror. He calls her again and again, his voice growing increasingly more desperate. Her throat is dry when she slips through the door and lets it close behind her.

Yasmin does not stop walking until she reaches the Weeping Woods. Her breath comes in heavy gasps, until a heaving howl climbs up and out of her throat. She bends and places her hands on her knees. Creatures gather round her, and the black quill appears in her hand, as though awaiting further instruction.

She straightens. It will not do for her subjects to see her like this. She lifts her chin, straightens her shoulders, sucks in a deep breath. Then she speaks.

"Hello, my loves," she says. The creatures growl and hiss and stomp. When they quiet, she hears a voice twirling in her ear. *Create*, it says, and the quill glows with a silvery light.

So she still belongs to someone. Is it relief or grief that knots her throat?

Yasmin lifts the quill. "Now we will create the most fearsome creatures the world has ever seen," she says.

She begins to draw.

August wakes on the ground. His eyes feel crusty, as though he has been asleep for many long days. He lifts his head and feels it pulse its pain in a nauseating wave. He puts it back down. He blinks up at the sky. His hand is touching another hand. It belongs to one of the other Lost Boys, as they have taken to calling themselves, a title of bittersweet proportions.

He tries again to lift his head. The world is hazy.

Where is he? He remembers…what does he remember?

With panic clawing at the back of his throat, August scrambles to his knees. He remembers a humming sound, like the wings of fairies. He did not see them.

He remembers the Lost Boys, their collective decision to depart from this foreign kingdom of Lincastle and return to their homeland of Fairendale, for the purpose of demanding that the king surrender his throne so that the rightful king could take his place. They believe the rightful king is Theo, the magical boy (and August's best friend) who saved the Lost Boys from the king's men the day King Willis ordered all the children of Fairendale captured in cages. Theo had led them here, to Lincastle, to a safe place where they could hide.

He remembers, too, the dreams—dreams that have left their terrifying mark on his chest. Were they real? Were they Visions? Or were they, simply, fantasy?

August looks around. The other Lost Boys are stretched out in varying positions on the ground. He shakes Ernest, the boy closest to him. "Get up," he hisses. "We must leave." Ernest opens his eyes, which have the same crust August wiped away from his. But August does not stop to wonder why. He moves to Henry, Leo, Norman. Fineas is last. Fineas stares up at him, the confusion plain on his face as he peels away the crust blinding him.

"We must leave," August says, looking around again. "Before they return."

"Who?" Fineas says, but August pulls him to his feet. He motions for the boys to follow him, to move back toward the village of Lincastle, where at least they will be safe from fairies.

But they do not get far. The fairies, who must have been there all the time, brighten into visibility. They form a ring so large around the Lost Boys that August shivers. He has never seen so many fairies before. They will never get through the lustrous line.

August feels his shoulders sag, feels the breath sag out of him as well.

The fairies glow in every color imaginable, and their faces—what faces the boys can see; there is a large army of fairies, and the Lost Boys cannot make out every one—are impassive, aloof, almost bored, as though not only do they mean no harm to these Lost Boys but they are also exceedingly uninterested in what they have come to do.

Perhaps it will not be as bad as he thinks.

Three days ago—or was it longer? He has been asleep; he does not know for sure—the fairies visited the Lost Boys, offering to carry them to a land where they would never grow up. Never Land. The boys stalled, asking for more time to think about this important decision. The fairies graciously gave them three days. As the third day neared its end, the boys fooled themselves into thinking they had been forgotten.

Fairies never forget. And now more fairies have

gathered—more than they have ever seen before.

The silence is so heavy August tries, in vain, to find something to say. His tongue feels heavy.

The boys wait. And the longer they wait, the more they tremble.

At last a fairy breaks rank, drawing nearer to the boys than the others. August recognizes her opaque green wings and the silken red gown with sleeves like miniature bells. Her green eyes whittle away at what courage he had upon waking—which was not much.

"Hello there," the green-winged fairy says. August tries to recall her name. Tara, he thinks it was.

She keeps her gaze on August. She says, "Did you sleep well?"

"Did we sleep?" Fineas says, the confusion plain on his face.

Tara laughs, a tinkling sound. When she is finished, she says, "You slept for three days."

August feels his knees weaken. He tries to remain on his feet.

"What did you do to us?" Fineas says. His voice is harsh. August thinks that he, perhaps, should have been the leader of these Lost Boys, not August.

Tara waves her tiny hand. "I only thought you might like to sleep on your decision." She lifts her chin. "And did you sleep well?"

The boys do not look at one another. August knows why. They saw the same things he did. Destruction. Death. A future, perhaps, that they did not want to live.

But how much of it was a trick?

August cannot be sure what draws the words from him, but he says, in a voice much stronger than he feels, "We will not go."

Tara nods, as though she is not the least bit surprised. "Well," she says. "The land of Never Land will miss you." She smiles now, a lovely shining one. "And this land?" She tilts her head. "It will not be glad you remain."

August looks around at the boys now. A couple of them don't meet his eyes, but Fineas does. He nods.

"We belong in this land," August says. "Not Never Land."

"Noble boys," Tara says. She does not sound impressed. "Or foolish ones? Only time will tell." She turns her back on the Lost Boys. She says, "I think they are foolish."

The fairies begin to move and dance in a languid circle, a colorful circle, a circle that—is it August's imagination?—tightens around the boys. And as the fairies dance closer, they glow brighter and brighter and brighter until the boys have to close their eyes; they cannot stand the piercing nature of that white light. They lift their arms to their eyes, blocking out every possible ray. They feel the heat on their cheeks and their necks and their chests.

And then it is over. August opens his eyes. The fairies are gone.

So, too, is Fineas.

The Enchantress and the Huntsman—that is, Theo —are camped out on the perimeter of Lincastle, inside the Wishing Woods. A flash of light draws both their gazes to the eastern ridge of the woods.

"What is that?" Theo the Huntsman says. He has never seen a light so bright, as though something is exploding in slow motion.

"I do not know," the Enchantress says.

"Magic?" Theo says. He stands up. The Enchantress rises as well, slower and more gracefully.

"Perhaps," the Enchantress says. A tendril of fear curls around the edge of Theo's mind. He and the Enchantress are in uncharted territory here, though they have been to Lincastle before, for another lost child of

Fairendale. They found the most recent lost child, a boy, inside the village—inside the woods, to be precise. He had been captured by the bookseller of Lincastle. It was unclear what the bookseller was planning to do with him.

Now the boy has joined five other lost children of Fairendale, only they are no longer children; they are blackbirds, tweeting in cages, arranged in a cart pulled by a white mare.

It may seem strange to you that Theo, another lost child of Fairendale and the magical one for whom the king of Fairendale issued his order to round up all the children, is here, inside these woods, transformed as a Huntsman. He did it for the preservation of his life, you see. After leaving August and the other lost boys in these very woods, tucked in a shelter fortified with a Protection spell, he transformed into his current body and face. He became a Huntsman for survival, but also something more—to save the kingdom and its people. He is traveling with the Enchantress to ensure that the children are, indeed, saved.

He is a man where he used to be a boy. All that remains of the son of Arthur and Maude and the brother of Hazel is his striking azure eyes. It is a wonder the Enchantress has not recognized them.

But perhaps she is also preoccupied with covering her

own identity.

Yes. The Enchantress has something to hide as well.

The Enchantress and Theo stare at the light for a while longer, and then the Enchantress turns back to the Huntsman. "Or perhaps it is the fairies."

Theo tries his best not to let his face reveal his worries. He does not know if he succeeds.

In their travels, Theo has experienced the dangerous magic of fairies. It almost stole his life, in fact. One never knows, when one encounters a fairy, whether one will live or die.

He thinks about the lost boys. He hopes they are well. He wishes he could slip away for a time, check on them without stirring the suspicion of the Enchantress. He hardly survived the fairy ring, and he is a sorcerer; what would happen to non-magical boys?

"Perhaps we should leave these woods," Theo says. He could be on the lookout as they leave. He could lead the horse, the cart with blackbirds, and the Enchantress around the perimeter, and meanwhile search for the boys he left in the care of August, his best friend outside of Prince Virgil.

The light continues to glow, brighter than the sun.

The Enchantress does not answer. Her eyes narrow, as though she is angry, and he wonders at this. Has he said something wrong? He often does, though he does not mean to. His frequent errors are likely because he is a boy playing a man. His father would know why he has upset the Enchantress.

How he misses his father.

The light blinks out, only blackness in its place. The Enchantress and Theo continue staring toward where it was, neither speaking.

After a time, Theo says, "Has the looking ball shown you anything?" The Enchantress usually lets him see what the looking ball shows, but since they captured this latest lost child she has said nothing about the looking ball.

She takes such a long time answering that he wonders if she heard him. But then she says, "It has shown me an egg." Her voice is crumpled up and bitter.

"An egg?" Theo says. It is true that they have chased some ridiculous visions in the looking ball—a dwarf, a giant wolf, some very old women. But an egg? How could a child have endured a Vanishing spell and reappeared as an egg?

The Enchantress shrugs, as though answering his unspoken question. "Perhaps you should look into the looking ball."

She says the words innocently enough, but they have

been traveling together for more than three weeks now. Theo knows her well. She is angry. She is afraid. And she is embarrassed, too, just a little.

He does not know what to say. He could look into the looking ball, but what if it shows him something different? Whose vision would they follow? They have been traveling somewhat uneventfully (with the exception of the run-in with fairies) from child to child with the help of a magical looking ball, which typically shows them one transformed child (or an untransformed child, as this last lost child proved) at a time and where that child is located, revealed in block letters above the child's head.

From where did this looking ball come? When Theo asked the Enchantress, she said she found it in the cottage she inhabited in the Weeping Woods of Fairendale. She said it was hers. Theo is not convinced.

What if it is all a game? Only one of these captives looked like a lost child of Fairendale, and he knew them all. He sat with some of them in magic lessons, though boys in Fairendale were not supposed to possess the gift of magic; it was considered a threat to the throne of Fairendale, since sorcery is the only requirement for ruling the land. Sorcerers, to those in Fairendale, are the most important men and women; ordinary people were precisely that: ordinary.

"Here," the Enchantress says, and she shoves the looking ball into Theo's hands. He does not have to decide what to say after all.

"I cannot awaken it," he says. Though he possesses the gift of magic, he cannot let her know. At least not just yet.

"Can you not?" The Enchantress does not look at him when she says the words. Theo feels his heart stutter. She knows?

He waits. The Enchantress does nothing. And just when he is about to animate the looking ball and give away his carefully kept (or so he thought) secret, the Enchantress waves her hand over the ball. It flashes to life with a green glow. Theo peers into it.

At first it shows him nothing.

After some minutes, the mist in the center gathers into something clearer. He squints. He tilts his head. He closes his eyes and opens them again. The vision remains unchanged.

It is an egg.

Theo shakes his head.

The Enchantress sighs. "I must admit, I had hoped it would be..." She does not finish what she is saying. She shakes her head, her hair a deep shade of scarlet in the dim light of the woods.

"An egg," Theo says again. He sits back on his heels. "Surely it cannot be a child."

"Can it not?" The Enchantress sounds as confused as he is. And tired, too. She likely wants to finish this quest as quickly as he does. He has not completely figured her out; he does not know if she is on the king's side or his side—she is not aware that he, Theo the Huntsman, is not on the king's side, since he was commissioned, like her, by the king to find the lost children. There is something about her eyes that tells him she has plans that differ from the king's. But what those plans are is anyone's guess.

The looking ball has gone dark. Theo shakes his head again. "It is playing a game," he says into the stillness.

"This is no game, Huntsman." The Enchantress's voice is loud, furious, fragmented. "It is magic." Is it his imagination, or do her shoulders slump a little?

"Could we find them on our own?" He says the words so softly they may not be heard.

But the Enchantress shakes her head and says, just as softly, "No."

"Your magic could show us," Theo says, and what he means is, *My magic could show us.* He is not entirely certain it is true, but is it not worth trying?

"How would we know the children?" the Enchantress says. "This last boy, Oscar, he was the only one who looked like he did in Fairendale."

The words slip inside Theo's heart and quicken it. "How do you know what he looked like before he vanished?" he says.

The Enchantress's face reddens. Or perhaps that, too, is his imagination; it has grown quite dim in this clearing. She says, "I made them a home in the woods. A shoe-shaped house. I saw all of them."

Theo lets it go at that, but he can tell she is hiding something. He feels a little hurt by this, truth be told. He stares into the fire he made for them. "So what will we do, then?"

The Enchantress stares into the fire for a very long time. At last she says, "Well, I suppose we will look for an egg."

Theo shakes his head but says nothing. When the fire begins to die down and the forest's evening chorus hums into being, the Enchantress leaves him for her tent. He remains, wondering, questioning, and, most of all, planning.

Prophecies

Matilda's daughter, Aleen, was three years old when the prophet Bregdon visited her again. This time he asked her to make a magical cauldron.

She was in the middle of tending a patient, laying out herbs over a leg wound. The patient, a large, burly man, was asleep on a mattress inside her sick rooms, which were tucked away in a detached structure off to the side of her cottage. The work gave her something to do, a barrier of sorts. She did not even have to look at the prophet.

The leg was badly mauled, a wound handed out by a wild animal of the woods. Matilda had never seen something so awful before. Once she finished laying out the herbs and bandaging the leg, she would hold her hands over it, too. Her magic was such that she did not need her staff to be in its staff form; it could remain the pearl choker around her neck for something as comparatively simple as healing. Though this wound was worse than others she'd tended. She might need her staff in its full form for this one.

The prophet waited. Matilda concentrated all of her magic into the hidden wound. When she felt the warmth swell and then subside, she put her hands down and turned to the prophet.

"I will not do it," she said. She could not create another magical object with the potential to be used for harm. She had a child to think about, after all.

"Because you are afraid." It was a statement, not a question. Bregdon took her hand. "Have you heard reports of the spinning wheel?" he said. "Has it been used for harm?"

She should have known she could not hide her fears from a man such as him. And it was true: she had heard nothing of an evil spinning wheel.

"The wheel is safe," Bregdon said. "I will keep the cauldron safe, too." He hesitated and cleared his throat. "Should you decide to make it." And then, after a breath: "You can trust me, Matilda."

Matilda knew this. But she had known others in her life who had said the same words, and where were they now? Gone.

She shook her head. "I cannot do it," she whispered.

"It will be used for great good," Bregdon said. He insulated her hand with both of his. His were warm and dry.

"What will it do?" Matilda said.

"It will bring the dead back to life. For one more chance."

"I do not have power over life and death," Matilda said. At least her answer would be simpler to explain this time. But the words caught in her throat. How she would like to be given that honor. She had tried once. She had failed.

"But you do," Bregdon said. He gestured to her patient. "You have just healed this man's leg."

She shook her head. "It is a wounded leg. It was not death." He would not have died because of the wound; he might simply have lost his leg.

"There are more ways to die than physically," Bregdon said. "You have saved this man's life."

She let the words settle into her chest. She could hear Aleen in the next room, talking to someone who was not there; the rest of Matilda's sick rooms were empty for now. Aleen was an imaginative child, and Matilda could picture her, so clearly, carrying on a spirited conversation with an imaginary friend. She smiled.

The prophet smiled, too, perhaps thinking her mind was once again made up. But she said, "Saving a life is not the same thing as bringing it back from death."

Bregdon's smile grew wider. "Oh, but you are wrong, Matilda," he said. "It is precisely the same thing."

She shook her head. Perhaps he was mad.

"What brought you to the Healing arts?" Bregdon said.

Matilda clenched her teeth. It was a trick question, but she answered it anyway. "Healing people," she said. "Offering them another chance at life."

She glanced at the prophet. His face shone.

After a moment, he said, "And something else too." And she knew that he knew.

Healing gave her something to do outside of her home. She had married young, a peaceful man who craved fame and fortune. He made ridiculous plans. She had tried to persuade him to stay here and live their small life, which was better than no life at all. He had gone anyway, six months before his daughter was born.

He had never returned.

Healing kept Matilda away from the eyes of the people. It kept her out of their thoughts. It kept her safe.

Matilda shook her head. "I am sorry I cannot help

you," she said.

"But it will be your gift as well," Bregdon said. He crept closer to her elbow. She was still not afraid. "When you die, you will be raised again. I have seen it."

The words shuddered into her, wrapped around her insides, and squeezed.

When you die, you will be raised again.

It was a promise, foretold by a prophet. This prophet. The one whose prophecies were as good as truth.

"Because of a magical cauldron," she said. It was not a question. It was a marvel.

"It will help many people," Bregdon said.

"And if it gets into the wrong hands?" Matilda said. She turned to look at him fully. "If the wrong hands use it to raise evil people?"

Bregdon shook his head. "We all have a capacity for good and evil, do we not, Matilda?"

Matilda could say nothing to this; it was true.

"There is always risk in anything we do," Bregdon said. And Matilda could say nothing to this, either; it, too, was true.

She knew she could trust this man, but she still did not know for certain whether she could trust his prophecies. What he had told her, however, was of the greatest importance. She would be raised from the dead.

She would have an opportunity to live again. He had seen it.

And is not immortality something for which every person longs? Matilda was only human.

So she made the cauldron. And the unfamiliar magical spell she wove over it was bright and brilliant and beautiful. It was the most magnificent act of magic she had ever achieved. It was a redeeming object, one that could bring hope and restoration. She was absolutely sure of that.

She had a very difficult time handing it over. But, in the end, she did.

Aleen wandered into the room as the prophet was preparing to leave. She pointed to the enormous cauldron he carried. "I am hungry," she announced.

Bregdon smiled and leaned down to tousle her hair, which was thick and knotted close around her face. "Hello Aleen," he said. She beamed up at him.

"What will you do with it?" Matilda said as she walked Bregdon toward the door.

"I will hide it," Bregdon said. "To be used in the distant future."

"When?" Matilda said.

"I cannot say for sure."

He had nearly disappeared through the door when he

turned once more. "You will do a great many things, Matilda," he said. "Your magic is very powerful. Just because you did not save your father does not mean you are weak."

So he had seen, then. She nodded and blinked hard and tried to believe him. She thought about asking him to try the cauldron here, now, since it might not work at all. But she pressed her lips together and watched Bregdon walk away, a slight bend to his shoulders.

What was it he carried?

Matilda heard Aleen behind her. "I am still hungry," the girl said. Matilda smiled and scooped her up.

"Then we shall eat," she said.

Aleen rewarded her with the loveliest smile.

Tactics

The first thing Yasmin does upon waking in the morning is draw herself a large and elaborate breakfast. She draws eggs and thick strips of bacon and fluffy white biscuits and pots of peppered gravy and fruit overflowing on white plates. She stares at the feast sitting on the throne room platform and feels her belly lurch. She will not be able to taste it, she knows, but that will not keep her from consuming. Which she does.

Once her belly is full of food that tasted of dirt and parchment, however, Yasmin is overcome with an overwhelming longing. A longing to do something, to be something, to shake the world as it has shaken her. She eyes the quill. She knows nothing about this quill, but she does know that there is always a limit to magic. What is the quill's limit? Should she test it?

Yesterday she drew creatures she remembered learning about long, long ago. They were released into the Weeping Woods. But her appetite was not satisfied. And as she slept, a wondering crept into her mind: Can she draw creatures that have never existed before?

She picks up the quill and tries.

Why, yes, she can.

The problem is that as soon as she draws a fearsome creature—one with six hairy arms and eyes on the ends of all those arms—it disappears from the throne room, as if the air consumed it. How odd. She tries again. The creature vanishes immediately. She tries again. This time the creature vanishes as she is drawing it, the lines erasing nearly as fast as she forms them. The quill is trying to tell her something.

She turns the quill over and over in her hands. Is it shorter than it was yesterday? She cannot be certain.

She rises from her seated position and paces in front of the platform, down below the stairs. She thinks. She is permitted to create the creatures, but not here in the throne room. Somewhere else?

Yasmin heads toward the throne room doors. She will attempt again, this time within the shadows of the forest.

It is a gray day, the kind of day Yasmin enjoys. Once upon a time she did not particularly enjoy gray days, but she is a new person, a new…well, she is not entirely sure what she is. She tosses these thoughts from her mind. No sense in raising more questions that cannot be answered.

(Had she once enjoyed questions that could not be answered? Who cares? she tells herself. And she tries to believe it.)

Inside the woods, Yasmin has no trouble birthing brand new monsters, hybrids of all the old ones. She marvels at this gift she has been given, the capacity of her mind to imagine such horror and the power of the pen to create it. She clearly sees the monsters in all their fearsome glory, her hand traces their lines, and they appear out of nothingness. She can even resize them if she wishes, make them larger or smaller depending on her desires (she mostly chooses larger). She laughs. She lifts the quill. She draws on air.

One after another she creates them: a giant lizard with an extra head on its pointed tail and feathered black wings that can sweep a fierce wind through the land (she calls this an Amphibaves); a large white bird with the face of a woman and fingerlike talons that can tear flesh apart (she calls this a Warpy); and a broad-boned bison with rounded horns thicker than a man's legs and a potent smell that explodes from its hind end at will (she calls this a Bonnacon; she mistakenly believes she invented it, but

Bonnacons have been around for a while in the larger world, just not in the land of Fairendale. If Yasmin had been exposed to a reference book about fearsome creatures of the world, she would have read about the Bonnacon and his deadly flatulence that can fell a whole field of mighty soldiers. We will let her have her fun.).

Yasmin has only just begun.

The sun is much higher in the sky—obscured by clouds, but still barely visible—by the time she is done, and the magical quill pen is decidedly smaller. Yasmin looks around at her terrifying creatures. The time, the expenditure of the magical pen—they were worth it.

"Come, my loves," she whispers, and they gather in a tighter circle around her. She is not the least bit afraid; they belong to her, after all. They will do whatever she commands.

It is good to have an army at her back.

Yasmin gazes up at the sky. She waits to hear the words she knows she deserves: *Well done.* But she hears nothing. The disappointment is sour in her mouth.

She does not need his affirmation to know that she has done well, does she? No. Absolutely not. She is her own woman—or…well, whatever. Yasmin turns back toward the castle. She will bring her creatures with her. The world will know her power, and it will tremble.

But as she crosses the boundary between the woods and the castle grounds, a creature cries out. Yasmin turns. It is as though they have all hit a solid barrier. They remain in a straight line, an imaginary line traced on an invisible wall.

Yasmin tilts her head and moves back to them. Is it simply an illusion? Can she dismantle it with her pen? She scribbles and slashes an X here and another there and stabs the pen into the wall she cannot see but all her creatures can feel. But no matter how hard she tries to destroy it, the wall remains.

Her confidence falters as a question invades her mind: Can it be that the beasts were born not to serve her but him?

"What is it, my loves?" Yasmin calls into the distance between her and the monsters. "What is keeping you from me? Come."

They try, but they cannot.

Yasmin returns to them, reaches out her hand to touch them, and gasps when they disappear. "My loves?" she calls. Her voice rises in anguish. Has she lost her masterpieces? No.

No, no, no, no, no!

She lunges toward the woods but meets something solid, like brick. Her shoulder screams, which makes her scream. When she reaches out her hand, her fingers brush a wall. Invisible but present. The same wall that kept her creatures inside the woods now keeps her outside.

Yasmin balls her fists and grits her teeth. She stares into the woods. She will find a way. She always has.

She traces the perimeter of the castle grounds, spending the better part of the late morning searching for a breach in the wall she can now, unexplainably, feel. She crosses a tributary, where she nearly drowns (she never truly learned how to swim, though she was originally from a land by the sea; the sea had never appealed to her even with its promise of sea monsters.). She passes the quiet village, keeping as close to the tree line as the invisible wall permits so she does not attract notice (she is not quite ready for the villagers to know about her). She moves past the castle gardens and all the way back around, but there is no opening through which she can slip.

She is a prisoner now.

Yasmin stops at the castle doors and looks back, squinting toward the woods, hoping for some movement that might indicate the presence of her creatures. All is still.

She is in such despair as she stumbles through the

oaken entrance that she does not notice the woman, large and tall and straight-backed, standing just outside the kitchen entrance to the castle.

And even if she did notice, she would not know that this woman is responsible for the wall that keeps her creatures out and, now, Yasmin in.

The monster is not as bad as Cook expected. She is not one of the walking dead, or at least not the kind Cook has met in her life. It is clear that the woman—who calls herself Yasmin—has been raised from the dead, but it is a different sort of raising, one that has been done by man, not the Grim Reaper—and that is an essential difference. Yasmin's eyes do not look as though they lead to death. She is fearsome, of course, but she is not deadly.

Yesterday Cook remained awake in her bed long into the night, pondering how Yasmin could have slipped through her protective spell, which was the strongest one she knew how to do. Perhaps it is because Yasmin is not completely a monster. She retains a bit of her humanity. Not much, but a glimmer. Cook has seen it. Yasmin has all the emotions of a human, which she displayed recently, while Cook watched outside the entrance to the kitchen, which looks upon the very stretch of woods where Yasmin tried to bring her creatures onto the castle grounds.

They could not breach the perimeter. And as Cook watched Yasmin try to dismantle the invisible wall, Cook said a few words, sent them toward the wall, and effectively banished the creatures deeper into the Weeping Woods and trapped Yasmin inside the castle grounds, separating monsters from their…leader? Cook shivers.

This separation will not last forever; Cook's magic is not strong enough for that. But perhaps in the short time (hours, likely) Yasmin is trapped the creatures will disburse and make it all the harder for Yasmin to gather them again.

Cook feels perplexed by the state of this protective barrier; it clearly works to keep monsters out, but there is still the matter of Yasmin. But she supposes the scrap of humanity that remains in Yasmin might be a loophole in the protective spell she used before leaving Fairendale castle on her last shape shifter assignment; she will learn from her mistakes. She will better protect Fairendale, with a stronger spell, the next time she is called away.

She thinks it will be soon. She has not wanted to consider it. She only just returned, and the boy only just recovered. She cannot leave him so soon, especially when there is a monster—with a wisp of humanity, but still a monster—inside the walls.

Cook shakes her head. So many questions beg to be answered. Who is Yasmin? Why has she come? How did she create such fearsome monsters? Cook has spent a good deal of time in the forests of the land, and she did not recognize some of those creatures. To be given the power of creation…

It is all baffling.

Magic is baffling.

Cook places her palm on her forehead. She wonders if she really saw all those creatures or if her eyes were playing tricks on her because she did not get her nap today after securing the walls of Fairendale castle. Perhaps she is simply tired. Perhaps Yasmin has no power whatsoever and does not know, herself, why she is here. Perhaps the feeling in Cook's chest—the profound heaviness—is only exhaustion, not a premonition.

She hopes it is so.

Cook sinks into a chair and rests her hands on her knees. She needs to think without interruption, and that means she likely needs to don her bearskin.

She does not want to leave the boy.

But she must, if only for a few minutes.

Cook sighs and rises again. She will tell Calvin to start supper on his own. It will be good for him to learn the ways of the kitchen, at any rate—how to make a proper loaf of bread, instead of a brick; how to choose the appropriate vegetables for soup, instead of cobbling together those that war one another for the dominant taste; how to store and stack the garden bounty so it does not spoil.

After all, she will not always be around to help him. She would like to be, but that is not the nature of life.

Every beginning has an end.

The old crone, who has remained on the porch of the house where she laid Maude to rest in a bed beside Hazel, notices that, by degrees, the woods have grown darker these last few hours. She stares into them for a time, squinting, opening her eyes wide, peering down her nose. She hopes it is her imagination. But she has lived long enough, and she has seen signs enough to know that no strange sight—the nearly imperceptible darkening of the woods by degrees—should be ignored; she will have to tell the others. Some cannot sense the play of light and dark, and she has always been very good at it.

She must stop whatever is causing this stealing of the light.

The crone moves toward Fairendale castle.

She has, for now, finished her work in the woods; the woman and the girl will sleep for a time, but they will be safe enough. She must turn her attention to the castle. Her throat tightens. She would rather not go back. But she must.

As she walks, the old crone transforms. She does not remain an old woman bent in two but becomes a straight-backed, golden-haired, sapphire-eyed young woman. A face and gown and hair befitting a princess or a queen or….well. She is impatient with remembrances; she has work to do.

But as soon as she attempts to step across the boundary line between the Weeping Woods and Fairendale castle, she slams into an unexpected wall.

It is unexpected because usually the woman—old crone or young beauty?—is able to detect the traces of magic, the shimmering edges of a spell, the slight hint of color that hangs between the spaces. But whatever this is —the wall—is completely invisible. There is no hint of magic here. The woman reaches out her hand and touches the wall. It is precisely that: a wall. She shifts a few steps to the side, her hand trailing it. She whispers some words, but the wall does not give. She presses hard against it, but it does not shift. It is immovable.

She stares at the castle for a moment. And then she summons every bit of her strength and tries, once more, to shove through the wall. She is knocked to the ground for her efforts.

The woman picks herself up and dusts off the dirt. She looks around. No one is here, and she is too far away from the windows of the castle for anyone to notice her.

Well. She will have to find another way in. She was always good at finding solutions and executing them. It is what has kept her alive for so long. If one knew her story, one would agree.

At last the woman turns back toward the woods, back toward the house of the Enchantress, but when, after an hour or so, she has almost reached the rim of the woods that widen into the clearing where the house sits, a strange feeling creeps down her spine. She immediately halts, stiffens, and turns around. Before her stands a creature she has never seen before, one with a lizard-like body, a snake-like tongue tasting the air, feathered black wings and an extra head on a pointed scorpion's tail that looks as though it can strike right through the heart of an opponent.

And that is precisely what it tries to do.

The woman, still in her youthful form, dodges and rolls, runs and lunges, pulls from her wooden belt a gleaming sword, a small dagger, and a wooden axe that, when her words meet it, lengthens into a thick, gnarled staff of almond-colored wood. At the top of this staff, iron claws twist around a clear crystal ball.

A looking ball? Perhaps. It is, for now, unclear.

The creature attempts another strike, but the woman is too fast, too nimble. She dives out of the way, rolls, and is on her feet before the creature can turn around. She plunges a blade into the creature's side. It squeals in pain and lifts its tail with the terrifying head, to strike again. She says, "Begone from here," and a blaze of rose-tinted mist wraps around the creature and carries it away—to distant lands, she hopes.

The woman bends, her breath coming in gasps. But she does not remain there for long. When she has caught only a fraction of her breath, she looks up to see more creatures for which she has no name. She touches her staff to the ground, and they vanish in a mist of rose. She runs, dodging through trees, and does not stop until she reaches the porch of the cottage where Maude and Hazel sleep. There the woman—old once more—assesses the damage done. She is satisfied to see that only a small tear in the hem of her cobalt blue dress tells of a struggle with a—what was it? She looks toward the place where the creature—the creatures—stood and uses her magical sight to see across the distance. A couple of trees lie on their sides. They will mend themselves.

A profound exhaustion sweeps over her, making her eyelids heavy. So heavy.

She cannot sleep on the porch. So the woman opens the door and enters the home of the Enchantress.

It was, after all, her home first.

In the village of Fairendale, Sir Greyson stands outside the cottage that belongs to Cora. He lifts his hand, as though to knock. He holds his hand in midair for a long moment. Then he drops it.

She does not want him here. The last time they saw one another…

He shakes the memory from his mind and straightens his captain's coat, which looks almost like a carpet, cut in a perfect rectangle, with holes for arms. It is a deep blue color that brightens his eyes. On the center of his chest, embroidered into the fabric, is a bear.

Sir Greyson has been captain of the king's guard since he was seventeen, and though he has returned to his mother in the last several weeks, sharing with her one of the small cottages in the village, he long ago gave up his civilian clothes. So he wears the black breeches and leather boots and long coat of the king's men.

He does not wear armor. He has no need of it anymore; he is no captain now.

Though, for a moment, he thinks he could use some armor around his heart. But it is only a fleeting thought; Sir Greyson has never been the kind to keep his heart walled off from others. Not even Cora. Not even when she has hurt him so terribly.

Sir Greyson lingers at Cora's door. His shoulders slump more than they used to—and for good reason. Before settling back here in Fairendale, Sir Greyson lost all the king's men to dragon fire in the dragon lands of Morad. He betrayed the king by choosing Cora. Then he betrayed Cora by...

No, he never betrayed Cora. He simply tried to keep her out of danger, and she did not want to be protected. He simply did not share everything he had to share, waiting for the right time and place and opportunity. He simply told the truth.

Sir Greyson lifts his hand again, and again he lets it fall to his side. Cora has not been truthful. She has been making secret plans that do not include him. She has visited the land of the dragons, where his men died, and for what purpose? She refuses to tell him. He can see that there are secrets in her eyes—more secrets than the ones she has already admitted: She killed King Sebastien, she transformed the prince into a blackbird, she is a sorceress, still.

It is this last secret that causes his heart to quaver.

She is a sorceress. She is not supposed to be a sorceress. She has a daughter. When the magical people of Fairendale have children, they pass along their gift of magic to those children. It is magic's way of limiting the number of sorcerers so they do not become overwhelming. It is the universe's way of balancing good and evil.

And now the balance is broken.

The only way Sir Greyson can reconcile this knowledge in his mind is by embracing the notion of dark magic. Dark magic is what would preserve magic in a sorceress who had a child, correct? And he has seen the darkness in her. He has trembled at it.

Is Cora dangerous? No. He has loved her for many years, and she has never been dangerous.

But King Sebastien—she killed him. How to reconcile that?

Sir Greyson shakes his head, trying to clear his

thoughts. But they cling to Cora. He sees her as he last saw her: red hair whipping around her face, dress tangled around her feet, eyes blazing as she told him she did not need him.

She does need him, though. He is sure of it.

Sir Greyson lifts his hand again. His knuckles nearly collide with the door, but he lets his hand fall once more. His shoulders fall, too.

He has already lost her. There is nothing else he can do.

He turns away from the door.

And because there is nowhere else for him to go (his mother is sleeping, resting peacefully, and she will not need him until supper), Sir Greyson heads toward Fairendale castle. The last time he saw the king, Sir Greyson refused a direct order: to arrest Cora. He chose Cora over his king's guard duties that day, and the king threatened his life—no, not just his life but both his and Cora's life. But Sir Greyson needs medicine for his mother, who suffers from the sugar sickness, and so he trudges on.

If he must lose his life for his mother, well, so be it.

Sir Greyson stands at the castle doors much like he stood at the door of Cora. There is a strange silence hanging around it, an eerie sort of hush that makes him feel as though he should walk right in, rather than knocking. Knocking would seem much too intrusive, and he still possesses his key. When the king threatened his life, he did not leave with Sir Greyson's key.

He slides it out of his front pocket and into the door, at the same exact moment a heavy sense of terror falls over him. It is too quiet. It is much too quiet. The click of the door opening sounds more like an explosion, echoing into the hall. He closes his eyes. What will he find? Have they all been slain? Is it only ghostly forms that remain in this castle now?

The hallway extending from the entryway is empty. Sir Greyson creeps in, careful not to make a sound with his boots. Perhaps he should have taken them off, but he is not entirely sure he is wearing socks without holes.

Sir Greyson moves first toward the throne room. He carefully peels open one of the doors, only enough to peer through with one eye. He expects to see the king inside, but, instead, he sees an unfamiliar person. A person? He opens the door a bit more, careful to avoid the angle that will make it groan. He squints his eyes. No, it is not a person. A monster? It is not quite a monster, either. He stares a moment longer. He tries to make sense of what he sees, but there is no sense to be made, so he backs away from the door, catching it so it returns to its closed state with nothing more than a slight whispering click.

No sense in startling the monster-person.

With fear and a storm of questions—what has happened to the king? Where are the other castle people? Why is the monster-person in the throne room, sitting on the throne?—driving his steps now, Sir Greyson walks much faster and much more purposefully—but no less silently—than he did before. He turns down the familiar hallways of the castle, headed for the king's chambers. He did not visit the king's chambers often, since a king usually prefers a throne room or a dining hall as the place where orders are given to his captain, but his memory has stored well the way.

Halfway there, he spots at the end of the hall a boy of about sixteen, perhaps. Tall, gangly, with a mop of brown hair folded over into his eyes. Garth, he remembers. The king's page. He is still here.

Sir Greyson's joy nearly brings tears to his eyes. He does not even know the boy. But he is so glad to see someone familiar here.

Garth has not noticed him.

"Excuse me," Sir Greyson calls. He presses his hand to his mouth, his voice still twirling in the hall, colliding with the walls. He did not mean to be so loud, but everything is loud in such extreme silence. He hopes the monster—or woman—did not hear him.

The boy looks up, his hair flying out of his eyes. Sir Greyson closes the distance between them. "Captain?" Garth says.

Sir Greyson smiles, heat rising to his face. "I am no captain any longer."

The boy does not seem to hear him. "I am so glad to see you, Captain," Garth says. And before Sir Greyson can respond, Garth rushes on. "There is a monster in the throne room and another in the mirror and the king is holed up in his chamber because that is the only place where he is safe and we do not know what to do about any of it."

Sir Greyson puts a hand on the boy's arm. "Garth," he says. Garth looks up. "I have come to see the king." Sir Greyson glances in the direction of the throne room. "I thought I might find him…" He does not finish, but Garth seems to know what he intended to say.

"The monster has taken the throne," Garth says.

"What kind of monster?" Sir Greyson says. "It looked like a person, too."

Garth shakes his head, one shoulder raising in a half-shrug. "We have never seen anything like her."

"Her?"

"She is…" Garth pauses. "Part woman, part living dead?" He looks at Sir Greyson, as though waiting for him to explain the duality.

Sir Greyson disappoints him, however. His heart is thumping much too hard. He manages to squeeze out, "The king is in his bedchambers?"

"Yes, sir," Garth says. "Along with the queen. I will take you to them."

Sir Greyson follows Garth. His steps sound like betrayal. Would a monster have overtaken the throne if he had been here, protecting the king as he vowed to do all those years ago?

Garth halts at the king's door. They arrived much sooner than Sir Greyson would like, but he says, "Thank you, Garth."

"You will find the king much changed," Garth says. Sir Greyson swallows hard and nods.

Garth knocks on the king's door and says, "Your Majesty."

King Willis, on the other side of the door, says, "Is that you, Garth?"

"Yes, Your Grace," Garth says. "And—" But Sir Greyson holds up a hand.

"Enter," King Willis calls.

Sir Greyson's heart seizes up.

Garth swings open the door.

Yasmin can smell him: an intruder. She tilts her head, closes her eyes, lifts her chin, and draws in a deep breath through her nose. He smells of fear and something else, something deep and hidden and sweet.

Love.

He smells of love.

It is all over him, it is wrapped around him, it is overwhelming. Yasmin would like to wrinkle her nose, but instead, she draws in another breath. It has been a very long time since she has smelled love.

For a moment, Yasmin is lost in a memory: a boy who used to sweep her cottage floors and smile at the table laid in front of him and talk endlessly of making her a queen. She never wanted to be a queen.

Yasmin glances toward the throne room mirror. King Sebastien has not appeared in it since she returned from the forest, and she must admit that she is glad. She does not want to see him again, at least not yet.

In her hands is the black quill. It is much smaller than it was originally; for every creature she created, the quill grew smaller. This tells her its magic is finite. And she might have created an army in vain; she has not been able to enter the woods to see if her creations still exist. Is there enough magic left in the quill to do it all again? And what would be the purpose of her efforts, if her creatures simply vanish as though they are made of nothing?

If she were not so melancholic, she would be angry. But angry requires energy she does not have.

Should she pursue the intruder? No. That, too, requires energy she does not have. She will allow him to remain in his delighted, love-filled state. He is insignificant. A wounded warrior who will do nothing.

She will let them all think they can make their plans, execute their plans, see their plans come to fruition. They will not win against her, the queen of the dark creatures.

Yasmin twirls the quill between her fingers. The corners of her mouth lift until she spies herself in the mirror. It is a ghastly sight. She laughs, but it is a hollow laugh, full of something she would never confess: sorrow.

Can a creature have a conscience? This one does. This creature feels sorrow for what has been and what is and what will be. This creature would do almost anything to be given a choice: live or die. The choice was made for her, and she is left with its consequences. It is a most tragic irony.

Yasmin reclines in the throne, lifting her legs and propping them over one of the golden arms. Her head rests against the other. She lets the cold soak her.

But no matter how much she enjoys the chill, it always wears off. Cold always warms.

It is the story of life.

Queen Clarion looks from Sir Greyson to King Willis and back again. Her gaze lingers on her husband. Her husband, but not quite. No, her husband from before. Before the throne's influence, before the mirror's control, before power and desperation and a crown twisted him and sucked away all the best parts of him.

Perhaps a monster invading the castle was the best thing that could have happened. She almost finishes the thought without a shudder, but it trickles down her back at the last moment.

King Willis has shed weight not just in physical pounds but in metaphorical, emotional pounds as well. He is—can she call him jolly? His cheeks flush pink and a white lock of hair falls over one of his earth-brown eyes. He brushes it away without much notice. The rest of his hair is still a sandy color. She supposes the lock of white is a mark of the dark magic.

He certainly looks happier.

How is he happier with someone else—a monster—sitting on the throne in his place? Queen Clarion has her suspicions; she believes the throne is driving most of the king's former cruelty. He has not sat on this throne in a day (has it only been one day? Queen Clarion feels as though time has stretched and expanded; one day has been a whole lifetime). And look at him now.

He is like the man with whom she fell in love, all those years ago. The man who searched for his brother. The man who was his own person and not the clone of his father.

She is so glad.

She still cannot quite figure out what the throne does to those who sit on it. Does it create illusions in their minds? Does it twist those minds into something unrecognizable? Does it wrap its dark magic around the one who would dare sit?

And what does that mean for the monster sitting on it now?

Queen Clarion tries to focus on King Willis and Sir Greyson. They are catching up. King Willis has asked about Sir Greyson's mother, even. She could see how surprised the captain was at this unexpected concern.

Yes. The old Willis is back.

Garth pokes his head in the door. "Would you like some sweet rolls delivered to your chambers?" he says. "Cook thought she could make a fresh batch."

The king shakes his head and says, "I would like some bread and butter, please, unless Sir Greyson would like some sweet rolls."

"Bread and butter would be wonderful," Sir Greyson says.

Queen Clarion stares at King Willis. Sweet rolls are his favorite food—or perhaps they *became* his favorite food, once the curse did its transformational work. Still, she moves to his side and presses her hand against his forehead. "Willis?" she says. "Are you feeling all right?"

King Willis nods his head vigorously, his hair shaking along with it, as though there is nothing else to say but yes. Yes, blissfully yes. Queen Clarion narrows her eyes and studies him—the way his eyes dance with silent laughter (though there is a monster sitting on the throne of Fairendale), the way his cheeks continue to glow pink, the way he looks so alive, so content, so unafraid.

Perhaps he is hysterical.

Or perhaps he is under some other kind of strange spell.

Queen Clarion swallows something cold and thorny.

She reaches out with her magic—which she has, regretfully, retained in place of the gift moving on to her son, the prince (she has never fully processed the implications of this and has chosen, for the last twelve years, not to think of it; there are always so many other things to consider.). She tries to feel what spell might hover over the king. She feels nothing.

The king shifts in his chair and crosses a leg. "It is so good to have you back, Captain," King Willis says. Queen Clarion watches Sir Greyson kneel before his king, and the sense of relief is profound in the chambers, as though it could be sliced into sections with a knife. Queen Clarion blinks her eyes and rubs her smarting nose.

She wishes she could feel that same sense of relief. But she cannot squash the alarm that continues to rise and ring in her. There is a monster on the throne, after all. Her son is not here in the castle but with all the villagers in some secret place. The lost children of Fairendale—not all of them, but some—are in the darkest place imaginable: the secret dungeons beneath the dungeons, and no one has been able to find the key to release them.

Perhaps the captain senses her unease. He glances her way and says, "I saw the monster on the throne." His eyes move back to the king.

King Willis's face darkens perceptibly, a shadow hovering around the eyes. Queen Clarion is both glad and reluctant to note the shadow: on the one hand, at least King Willis knows there is a problem; on the other, she hates that there is a problem at all.

"Yes," King Willis says. He looks down at his hands, twines them together. "There is a monster."

"Tell me what happened." Sir Greyson's voice is gentle. He leans forward in his large forest-colored wing chair. Though it swallows him, he looks regal, noble, efficient.

The king stands to his feet, unconcerned that he remains in his dressing gown, a robe tightened around his shrinking waist. He paces the room. Queen Clarion notes, with some surprise, the way he is shrinking and yet the way it makes him appear larger than before. It is as though he is stretching up, not out.

Queen Clarion has not seen her husband in many days. She has been preoccupied with her work in the castle library, where she has scoured, day and night, every book of magical studies that is in it. She is trying to learn how she might destroy the throne and the mirror. She would like both of them removed from Fairendale castle, but she does not think it will be a simple task, such as carrying them out and leaving them in the forest. They are dark magical objects; dark magical objects must be protected from those with a bend toward dark magic.

She must destroy them completely.

But she has found nothing, in all her days and nights of searching. Nothing in the histories or the magic tomes or the almanacs.

Her eyes feel so heavy they begin to droop. She startles back awake when the king says, "She wandered in. And that was that."

"From where did she come?" Queen Clarion says.

King Willis meets her eyes, and his hold a small scrap of fear, right in the center. "I did not stay in the throne room long enough to ask," he says. "I fled here."

Queen Clarion stares at her hands. There must be some explanation for this person—this monster. This… whatever she is. They must find it.

"What kind of creature is she?" Sir Greyson says. "I have never seen anything like her."

King Willis shakes his head and then nods it, as though agreeing with Sir Greyson.

"There are dead who live again." The two men turn their heads to Queen Clarion. She blows out a breath. "They are called Black Eyed Beings. They form the Grim Reaper's army and accompany him to collect the dead."

She tries not to acknowledge the look of horror that crosses both their faces.

"And you believe she is one of them?" Sir Greyson says. His voice is thick and low. She wonders if he is thinking of all his men, whom he lost to dragon fire. "You believe the Grim Reaper might be here?"

Queen Clarion chooses her words carefully. "I do not know if the Grim Reaper is here. She is somewhat different from the pictures I have seen of the Black Eyed Beings." She gestures toward her right eye. "They typically have spidering veins gathered in sunbursts or some kind of pattern. The creature does not have that."

Sir Greyson stares at the floor. "So she is not a Black Eyed Being," he says.

"She may be," Queen Clarion says. "She looks as though she has died and lives again."

Sir Greyson nods. He does not look any less confused than he did moments ago. Queen Clarion sympathizes; she feels confused as well. No explanation fully explains her—it—whatever the creature is.

They are silent for some moments. Only their breaths, the steady drawing in and expelling out of air, fill the chambers.

At last, Sir Greyson clears his throat. "I believe you must flee this castle," he says. "We do not know what the monster intends. We do not know if it is safe to remain."

Queen Clarion's heart clenches. She cannot leave the library. It is the largest library in the land, and if she is going to find what she must—she must!—find, it will be here. She must keep looking. She is about to shake her head when the king says, "I believe you are correct."

The king and the captain launch into a plan for escape, practically talking over one another in their haste to solidify details. Queen Clarion shakes her head. She is sorry to contradict them. She wishes she could go.

She says, "I cannot leave." Both heads turn in her direction.

"You must," King Willis says. It is not an order; it is an entreaty. She appreciates that; he is the old Willis now, no longer ordering her to do what he wills.

A heavy weight slides into Queen Clarion's chest. Her words come out a whisper: "My son." The eyes of King Willis grow glassy.

Sir Greyson kneels beside Queen Clarion now. She did not know his eyes were so arrestingly blue, like those of her father's. "Your son is safe," he says.

"You told me as much when I came to the village," Queen Clarion says. "But do you know where he is? Will he remain safe?"

She watches something shift in Sir Greyson's eyes.

She cannot read what bothers him; she does not know him well enough. She can see, however, that he is considering his words, carefully choosing those he thinks will soothe her mother heart. He says, "Prince Virgil is in the secret underground passageway that exists in Fairendale." He takes in a breath and lets it out. "I cannot tell you where it is. It would be a betrayal of the people, you see."

Queen Clarion nods, her eyes filling and spilling down her cheeks. Sir Greyson looks as though he regrets even the few words he said, but Queen Clarion presses his hand, hoping that he will read her message in her eyes: *Thank you.*

She does not say that both she and the king know about this secret passageway, that when they were young and audacious and unburdened by the reality of their worlds, Cora took both her and King Willis—then only a prince—to the secret passageway. They have been inside, they have lit its torches, they have made secret childish plans.

And now her son is there. She is glad. He will be safe.

She should have known, when the village people of Fairendale stormed the castle weeks ago to pilfer what food remained and demand that King Willis free their children who were locked up in the dungeons beneath the dungeons, the same day they took her son hostage, that they would keep him in the secret passageway. The passageway has a secret door, much like the one that guards the way to the dungeons beneath the dungeons (it is, in fact, the same kind of door, though Queen Clarion does not know it), and it does not allow intruders, only those it permits inside.

"So we could flee to the village," King Willis says.

The captain's face pinches a little. He clears it quickly, but Queen Clarion notices. "I do not know if that would be wise," he says. "Perhaps somewhere farther away. Lincastle, or Rosehaven."

King Willis nods as though he understands. And she can see, by the regret that sparkles in his eyes, that he does. He has, after all, stolen the people's children. Not one child remains in the village, as far as they know; it is why the kingdom of Fairendale no longer flourishes as it once did.

Queen Clarion very nearly swallows the words as she thinks them, but they come out before she can stop them. "Perhaps you are strong enough to beat the curse," she says.

King Willis shakes his head. "I think we can all agree that my past has not proven this." He clears his throat, a short bark of emotion.

"So there is a curse," Sir Greyson says. "On the throne."

Queen Clarion nods.

"My mother told me as much," he says. "I hoped I could believe her." His eyes drop to the floor. "She is very unwell."

"You must take her some medicine," King Willis says. "From the castle store."

Sir Greyson nods.

They lapse into silence again, all of them thinking. After a time, Sir Greyson says, "It is too dangerous for you to remain here. We will get you safely out, and then we will plan what comes next." He rubs his chest, as though brushing away some invisible pain, and looks at the king. "But we must leave straightaway."

King Willis gazes out the window cut out of his back wall. "I have always loved this castle," he says, his voice soft. "Though it does not hold the best memories for me." He turns and looks at Queen Clarion. "But some of them…" He lets the words trail off. Queen Clarion feels a warmth bloom in her chest.

"Perhaps leaving will not be forever," Sir Greyson says.

King Willis nods. "Perhaps you are right." He does not look like he believes the words, even as he says them.

His eyes are far, far away when he says, "Pack what you might need, Clarion. And we will go."

Queen Clarion does not argue this time; she has no energy left to do so. She is tired of fighting, exhausted of her search for answers. She stands and has nearly turned away when King Willis does something entirely unexpected: He embraces Sir Greyson. Queen Clarion watches the surprise skip across the captain's face, watches his eyes press closed, watches the tear drop from a corner.

And she knows, surely and certainly: Sir Greyson is a man who can be trusted, a man with honor and dignity and a thousand regrets, a man driven by love.

And love has always been enough.

Explanations

Two years later, the prophet returned.

Aleen was five. Matilda was twenty-seven.

"I need you to make a throne," Bregdon said when Aleen skipped off to gather some herbs on the edge of the woods.

"What sort of throne?" Matilda said.

"A magical one."

Matilda was growing tired of these evasive answers. "I could have guessed as much," she said, inserting into her voice a bit of an edge. She shook her head. "I will not make it."

She crossed her arms over her chest and leveled at the prophet her most challenging gaze. Or at least she hoped it was challenging. His eyes glittered back at her, like he was not the least bit unsure that she would, in the end, make that for which he had come.

"Tell me what you want." His voice was gentle.

"I want to know what you plan to do with these items I have made," Matilda said. She lifted her chin.

"Alas, I cannot tell you all I have seen," Bregdon said. Matilda was just about to tell him that if he could not share freely what he was going to do with these magical items, she was done with helping him and would not be able to make this requested throne. But before she could open her mouth, he continued: "But I am permitted to tell you some." He glanced around him, as though someone might burst into the room, but no one did.

A cold feeling spread down Matilda's back. Was he afraid of someone? Had he placed her and Aleen in danger because of what he was asking?

"This magical throne will have the ability to tease out darkness or light," Bregdon said. "It will bring out the best or the worst in a ruler."

"And why would you want to do that?" Matilda said.

She had not phrased her question correctly, for Bregdon said, "You can understand, perhaps, why we would want to bring out the best of a ruler."

"But the worst," she said and waited.

The pause was heavy.

"Well, it is good to root out the bad so that one might

be healed," Bregdon said at last. It was not an answer. It was another evasion.

"But an evil ruler becomes more evil," Matilda said. "And more impossible to defeat."

"Perhaps that is so," Bregdon said, and the cold spot on Matilda's back turned into an encompassing cloak. "But evil has its purposes, too."

Matilda stared at the prophet. How could he say such a thing? Evil did not have a purpose that she could see. Who was this man? What did he want?

"It is difficult to explain," Bregdon said.

"I would like you to try," Matilda said.

Bregdon nodded and took a deep breath. "Evil is a curse, something that can be seen by certain sorcerers. It can be…" He paused. "Extracted."

"Extracted how?" Matilda said.

"With magic. A magical throne, to be more specific."

Matilda tilted her head. "You mean this throne might, in the end, destroy the evil in a person?"

Bregdon nodded. "That is my hope."

And what were his hopes worth? Matilda studied him for a very long time, and what she found was that his hopes were everything.

Was a world without evil possible?

Matilda glanced toward the door, through which her

daughter would be bursting soon. If the possibility existed, if she, Matilda, could create a world in which evil did not have a place, a world where her daughter would know only goodness and not pain and fear and sadness—would she do it?

Yes. She would.

"And what of the other items?" Matilda said.

"Whoever possesses all three items at the same time, whoever brings them together, will have the ultimate power over life and death," Bregdon said. "The possessor will battle the Grim Reaper for souls that should be alive instead of dead." He seemed so untroubled by this alarming admission. Matilda shivered.

"Why would you give someone such power?" Matilda said.

"Because it will be the right person," Bregdon said.

"But how can you know?"

"I have Seen."

"The future is always changing," Matilda said.

"Yes," Bregdon said. He stroked his chin. She noticed that his nails were clean and cut. "The future *is* always changing." He fixed his strange eyes on her. "But does that mean we should inhibit the present possibilities because the future is uncertain?" He let the words sink in, and Matilda could think of nothing to say. He continued.

"Sometimes prophecy is not a gift at all. Sometimes it is an excuse not to take a risk."

"But a risk like this…"

"You have no faith in good triumphing over evil?"

Matilda thought on this for a moment. She had not seen much of that in her land. There were people who had come searching for diamonds in the snow-covered fields of White Wind, and they had practically torn the village apart at times. That was evil. People were suspicious of magic and all that was extraordinary about the magical world because of it. That was evil. She had to keep the full extent of her gifts hidden, settling for a smaller version of herself; that was evil, too.

It seemed that, at least for now, evil ruled the day.

She did not know what to say to Bregdon, and so she said nothing.

Bregdon leaned close. "A war is coming, Matilda. A war that will claim innocent lives. Lives that must be given a chance to live again."

Matilda shuddered at the prophet's words. "When?" she said. "When will this war come to our land?" It was always the missing piece: when. It could be in her lifetime, it could be much later. It could be tomorrow.

"I cannot say exactly when," Bregdon said, and Matilda remembered that prophets were not permitted to say when. Most of them were not even permitted to See when. They only knew that something was coming, and that was the best they could do with their Visions.

Bredgon's face was pressed into an expression of sadness. "I only know that it is coming. And we must all be prepared. We will know the signs when we see them."

"See them?" Matilda said. "How will we see them?"

"Strange things will happen in the realm," Bregdon said. "People will disappear. Dragons will walk the land again. Death will live." The prophet's eyes had turned milky. His words did not make sense. So went prophecy. It was often hard to understand. But his voice was strong, unwavering, certain. "There will be dangerous creatures, and there will be walking spirits, Black Eyed Beings, and the Grim Reaper..." Bregdon gave a shuddering breath, and his eyes cleared. He shook his head, as though to clear it, too. "That is all I know."

It was enough.

And yet, there was something. "What about those who deserved death?" Matilda said. "Will they live again as well?" Matilda's heart beat wildly, like a flailing child in her chest. She had cursed the man who had wounded her father many years ago, and he had died. She did not want to see him again, if only for the protection of this secret.

"Does anyone deserve death?" Bregdon said, and Matilda's stomach twisted.

They were silent for some moments before Bregdon said, "The items, when collected by the same person in the same place, will give their possessor the power over life and death. Their possessor will be able to bring back whomever he or she desires, no matter if they have already lived more than one life through the magical cauldron you made. The dead will walk out from a mirror." He seemed delighted by this prospect.

Matilda had another point to press. "And what if all three of these magical objects fall into the wrong hands?" she said. It was always the question, was it not?

"Perhaps they will for a time. There are many holes in the Vision I have been given."

"Then why follow it?"

"It is the only way," Bregdon said. "One cannot question the Vision one sees."

"What if there are others creating these objects?" Matilda said.

Bregdon smiled at her. "I saw you create them."

"Which means others have as well," she said.

Bregdon did not argue with this, and Matilda's heart beat faster. Would someone come looking for her? Would Aleen be in danger because of Matilda's foolish acts?

And had they been so foolish?

Her mind was a muddle.

"Where is the mirror?" Matilda said.

"It has not yet been created," Bregdon said.

"How will the dead be released, then?"

"Some spirits, those who may have died prematurely or because of a tragic mistake, are trapped in a realm removed from this one. Some say they are trapped in magic mirrors." Bregdon smiled with his crooked, old teeth, which were surprisingly white. "Some say there is one mirror that becomes a doorway."

It all sounded like nonsense to Matilda, but what did she know of magic and futures and the walking of spirits? She was a simple, untrained sorceress from White Wind. She had never even been out of the village.

"Why have you come to me?" Matilda said at last.

"Because you have been chosen," Bregdon said. And it was these words, not the accompanying, "Now will you make the throne?" that prompted her to say yes.

It was a lovely throne, made of smooth shining gold, with jewels of all colors lining the sides and top. The padded seat was of the deepest blue.

Though he was an old man, Matilda was surprised to see that Bregdon had no trouble carrying the throne away.

He was an enigma.

Disappointments

Arthur and Zorag sit around a fire outside the dragon land of Gyria, near the wasted land of Ashvale, thinking about all that has transpired. They have now visited two of the six dragon lands (not counting Morad, which is where Zorag is king). They have begged the dragons to join their cause—to make sure that the human race and, by extension, the dragon race are safe from the evil king of Fairendale (they do not know, yet, that there are other, more evil forces at work now). To ensure freedom. To restore the balance of light and dark magic in the realm.

None of the dragons have joined them.

It has been many days since Arthur and Zorag have heard news from other lands, since Gyria is well removed from the sounds and life of civilization. Ashvale, along with all its people, was destroyed years ago in the eruption of a Fire Mountain, which Arthur is still trying to reconcile. The Fire Mountains, Zorag told him (and Arthur has now witnessed), are not Fire Mountains at all. They are dragons—dragons who spit liquid fire that appears red upon first contact with air but, with time, dries into black rock.

Arthur ponders the news he heard the last time he visited a village—Rosehaven, the village that looks on magic with suspicion and distaste; the village where his children, Theo and Hazel, were born; the village from which he and Maude had to flee after welcoming magical twins (all the most powerful sorcerers in existence were twins) into the family. He heard there, from an old friend, that King Willis had sent word to all the kingdoms demanding they hand over their children. The demand might have been ignored, if not for the large reward attached to it. Arthur's friend said there were many in the kingdom of Rosehaven who would hand over their children for money.

Such ill-gotten gain.

Arthur's heart has tightened around this news every day that has passed. He would like very much to return to Fairendale, to plead with the king, to make him see reason, to change his mind. Perhaps to say more.

And there is also the matter of his lost family. He

thinks of them often. Are they safe? Are they well? Are they alive, even?

Maude will have done what she can to protect them.

Maude.

The longing throbs in his chest.

His hopes, perhaps, had been too high. He had wanted the dragons to join his cause in liberating the people, which, to him, meant a liberation, too, of the dragons. The dragons did not seem concerned with liberation. They did not seem bothered by their supposed exile; most of the dragons had never been friends of the people anyway, not like the dragons of Morad had been. The dragons of Morad had once upon a time worked side by side with the people, building the kingdom of Fairendale, ruling the dragon kingdoms from Morad, keeping peace in the lands.

The world has become a shocking mess.

Zorag has been moping. Arthur has been staring. Neither has been speaking.

Nearly two days have passed, and now, at last, Zorag speaks—grumbles is a better word for it, perhaps.

"We should count our losses now," he says.

"We do not have any losses," Arthur reminds him. It is a technicality worth pointing out. There has been no loss of life—and that is something to be celebrated.

Arthur and Zorag were not exactly welcome in the dragon lands they visited.

Arthur knows that Zorag has risked much in these last few weeks. He has not been the dragon king of the realm that he should have been, the one his father had been before him. He wrestles with both guilt and disappointment. Neither is easy.

It is because of Zorag that the dragons have not joined their cause.

No, that is not entirely true. There was Zorag's uncle (Zorag did not even tell Arthur that the king of Eyre was his uncle; Arthur is still a bit peeved about that). Rezedron, Zorag's uncle, would likely have joined their cause had he not been dying from a dark curse he picked up from the thorn of a white rose in Rosehaven. But the dragons of Gyria, the dragon land most recently visited, refused in a matter of minutes and threatened Zorag and Arthur with their lives if they did not depart the land immediately.

Which brought Arthur and Zorag here, to the woods somewhere between Ashvale and Morad.

"Why do you not command the dragons to fight with you?" Arthur has never asked this question before.

"That would be futile," Zorag says. "No one has ever won a war by demanding his subjects fight."

"But King Sebastien did," Arthur says.

"King Sebastien possessed something that I will never have," Zorag says. "Charm."

Arthur says nothing. He feels as though he has had this conversation before, and perhaps he has. Time is fluid and circular in upheaval. He is surprised, perhaps again, that the dragon knows about King Sebastien's charm, but he should not be. King Sebastien was, after all, responsible for the exile of the Morad dragons—and all dragons everywhere. They were even written out of storybooks.

Zorag and Arthur lapse into an uncomfortable silence until Zorag says, "I suppose we might only have the dragons of Morad with us." The disappointment is clear in his eyes.

"And they will fight?" Arthur asks the question gently. He does not want to upset the dragon further.

"They will follow me."

"Their number is small," Arthur says.

"They are strong," Zorag says.

Arthur presses his lips together, to keep from asking the question that nearly climbs out anyway: Are they strong enough?

Zorag seems to sense what he is thinking. He releases two puffs of smoke from his nostrils and turns away from

Arthur.

"I do not want to see dragons die," Arthur says. The words feel thick and heavy in his mouth.

"War always demands death," Zorag says. He pauses. "Though I do not, either."

They sit in a more comfortable silence than the last one, until Arthur says, "Perhaps we should seek the children ourselves."

"You think that would not start a war?" Zorag says. The dragon does not look at Arthur. "After the king's proclamation?"

Arthur feels a wrenching in his chest. The dragon is right, of course.

Where are they? Will he ever see them again? How will this all end?

"Would people be easier to mobilize than dragons?" Arthur is thinking out loud.

"And why would they join us?" Zorag says.

"Justice," Arthur says.

"The people I know never cared much about justice."

"Perhaps not all of them do," Arthur says. "But some of them, surely."

"Some is not enough," Zorag says, and he lays his head back down on one of his forelegs. "We need all."

Arthur's head hurts. He rests it on the dragon's other

foreleg.

"There are still more dragon lands," Zorag says. "We will finish what we set out to do. And if the dragons will not join us, we will move without them."

Arthur closes his eyes, trying to pretend that it was confidence, not fear, that he heard in the dragon's voice.

Yasmin walks the woods.

She managed, finally, to enter them today and spent hours locating her creatures strewn about the woods; she was glad to know they had not disappeared for good.

She has attempted, again, to bring some creatures onto the castle grounds, but the invisible wall holds. She finds this exceedingly strange. She is a creature herself; why is she permitted to walk the grounds while those who follow her are not?

Several times she has tried, and every time her creatures collide with a barrier that cannot be seen.

Yasmin is, to say the least, perturbed. Though she knows it is not time to execute the plan the Grim Reaper is slowly unfolding in her mind, the longer she spends in the throne room of Fairendale castle the closer she comes to remembering her humanity. Remembering is a dangerous thing; she has been given a purpose, and without that purpose, who is she?

This line of thinking, of course, raises more questions than answers. Who is she even with this purpose? Is she Yasmin, or is she the woman with dancing eyes who stood by a fire and cooked for a family? Is she creature or woman? Is she both? And how can this be?

The questions plague her inside the walls of the castle. She wanted a creature to bring back with her, thinking a creature would remind her of her purpose and would effectively halt the remembering.

Yasmin paces. The creatures have scattered into the Weeping Woods, as she commanded them to do ("Stay close, and multiply," she told them). She considers calling them again, to perhaps try again, but before she can release the magical words, an old crone limps out from behind some trees. She has gnarled hands that clutch a walking stick, on which she leans heavily. Her rutted skin and snow-white hair speak of age and wisdom. Her milky eyes seem to see nothing. Yasmin watches the woman, who is near bent in two, pat the ground with her almond-colored walking stick.

If Yasmin says nothing, the old woman would not know she was even here.

But curiosity gets the best of her. Curiosity and

something else: jealousy. What is this old woman doing walking in her woods? Yasmin stands straighter. She is a good four heads taller than the old woman. And she can see.

"What are you doing in my woods, old woman?" Yasmin's voice hurtles into the stillness of the trees. The old woman does not startle, which is surprising. But then, when the old woman does not answer, Yasmin wonders if, perhaps, she is deaf as well as blind.

She tries something else: "Are you lost?"

The woman does not answer.

And one more time. "What would you do if I transformed you into a slithering snake with my magic quill?"

Still nothing.

So she allows the old woman to pass. She is no threat. The old woman passes so close to Yasmin that Yasmin can smell her age and a minuscule hint of cinnamon. But the woman does not glance at her, does not even acknowledge that she has noticed anyone at all in this forest.

Yasmin shakes her head and moves on. She is done with pacing. She heads back toward the castle.

A dragon flies past overhead; she feels the shadow before she sees it. She looks up and catches a glimpse before the creature is lost among the treetops. A black dragon, with a puff of smoke trailing after him. An angry dragon.

Well. Dragons will be no match for her creatures. She smiles. It shakes.

When she is almost back to the castle grounds, Yasmin hears the voice. *Summon the king*, it says. *Involve him in your plans.* The king. Which one? But the voice does not answer.

Yasmin considers.

Since the voice did not specify, she will choose King Willis. He is less…(she wants to say frightening, but she will not allow herself to say it)…demanding than King Sebastien. And, besides, he is the true king, for now. She tells herself this is enough.

As she strides across the castle grounds, she thinks of this king. He is weak. There is a glow of hope in him. That must be quashed. But first she must lure him from his chambers.

Which she will do with food.

She enters the castle as though it belongs to her. She heads toward the throne room, her hands searching the two pockets hidden by the folds of her dress. She stops.

Where is the quill pen?

Did she drop it? She retraces her steps, all the way

out to the woods and farther still, but she cannot remember her exact path. Her fists ball up. She peers into the dim spaces between trees. She grits her teeth and thinks.

It was the woman. It must have been. Yasmin placed the quill back in her right pocket after attempting one last barrier break with a Manticore (this was a creature from Yasmin's imagination that was a cross between a human, a lion, and a scorpion; she chose this creature to accompany her to the castle, but the wall, predictably, prevented its passing). She had no holes in her pockets. The woman was more than she seemed. Yasmin should have known.

Yasmin lets out a long sigh. Hope is not lost (is it ever?). She enchanted the quill with a Possession spell, which means it will return to her and, also, no one else will be able to use it. She will simply have to wait for its return.

She was once good at waiting. She will be good again.

Yasmin returns to the throne room and rings a silver bell, which she assumes is the servant bell. A boy scampers in, and she tries to ignore the fear on his face. She sends for the castle cook.

The woman who enters is much larger than any Yasmin has ever seen. She is not a giant, but very nearly.

Her wispy white hair frames a pale face and startling blue eyes. Yasmin cannot tell if she is young or old; the hair is old, but the body and face look young.

"You are the cook at this castle?" Yasmin says.

"Yes," the woman says.

"Has the king eaten this evening?"

The woman shakes her head. "No," she says.

Yasmin notices almost immediately that the woman does not address her by madame or Your Majesty or any title befitting a queen. She tries not to let it bother her.

"Prepare us a supper," Yasmin says. "I shall dine with the king."

"Very well," the woman says.

"All the king's favorite foods," Yasmin says. "I will eat the same."

She sends the woman away and drops into the throne, to wait.

Always waiting.

In the middle of the Weeping Woods, the old crone who met the monster-woman in the woods (whose name, of course, is Yasmin) holds up the stolen black quill pen and squints at it. She runs her fingers along its sharp feathers. She folds it into a pocket of her tattered dress and limps along her way, the walking stick keeping time in the quiet pulse of the forest.

Who is she? We have met her before.

To follow her movements would be to notice that she flickers in and out of focus, sometimes appearing as a bent old woman, sometimes appearing as a young woman with golden hair and sapphire eyes and not a wrinkle on her pale face. She looks like a lost princess.

And it is true that once upon a time this old crone was, indeed, a princess.

But it is not yet time to tell her story, and, besides, her flickering has ceased. It has culminated into a rose-colored glow, a flash, and a return to the bent-in-half body.

For good? Only time will tell.

Perhaps it is self protection. Perhaps it is something more.

She shuffles toward the house of the Enchantress, where she has been residing while Hazel and Maude sleep through dreams and wonderings and Visions much like those of prophets.

The Enchantress is in a black mood. She can feel it, hanging directly over her head, like a storm cloud that follows her no matter how diligently she tries to flee it. Every time the Huntsman talks, she snaps.

He has grown cautious with her now.

"Would you like me to get us some supper?" he says, tentatively, as though he is afraid of her, as though he knows that what is coming will be pointed and sharp. She cannot blame him; she has been unable to shake this mood for the last day.

An egg. They are searching for an egg. It is ridiculous. The looking ball is making fools of them; she is sure of it. She should toss it into a stream, and she would do that if she were not afraid of who might pick it up. Looking balls can be used for evil just like any other magical object.

It is safest to hold on to it. But she has been trying and trying and trying to think of a better way to find all the lost children. Why must their quest depend on a magical ball? Why did she ever think it was a good idea to take this from her cottage—*her* cottage, though she had never lived there before; why had she thought it was her cottage? Why had she thought this was her looking ball?

The Enchantress has begun questioning everything.

She sighs, a long, heavy, exasperated sigh. The

Huntsman opens his mouth as though to speak, but she holds up a hand. "It is not you, Huntsman." She lets it sit for a moment, lets it sink in. This is the closest he will get to an apology. The Enchantress has never been good at apologizing, at admitting any bit of weakness.

A profound weariness sweeps over her. She sighs again. She does not know what else to say, so she lets the air breathe between them. She tries to swat away the black cloud. She tries to find a bit of the energy with which she began this quest.

She is so exhausted. Her magic has been demanding more and more of late. She has even had doubts that she will finish this quest.

In her darkest moments of doubt she studies the Huntsman, tries to figure him out, tries to see the honor and courage in him. There is plenty of it. She has grown to like him during these travels—perhaps she even loves him, though she would never admit this aloud.

Still, it would not do to bring him into her plans. But she can discern, by some unsettling look in his eye— which is familiar, she must admit—that he does not plan to adhere to the king's orders for these children (though what were the king's orders? She cannot remember. She was so focused on the children at the time; she regrets she did not completely hear out the king. He is a wordy man, and she has never had the patience for men who like to hear themselves talk.).

The Enchantress has not peered into the looking ball since the egg showed itself so clearly last eve. She hoped that the Huntsman would see something different, and then she would have argued for a time about which vision they should follow, though she would know all the while that they should follow his. It is ridiculous to believe that a child was transformed into an egg.

And what kind of egg is it? She cannot tell. She never liked scientific studies; she preferred only the instruction in magic, though her mother had demanded she at least read about the other subjects. The Enchantress had never done well in those other studies, but she had excelled in sorcery.

Which contributed greatly to her current circumstances.

And yet her excellence in sorcery cannot help locate the lost children of Fairendale. Why not? She encountered an old crone in the Weeping Woods of Fairendale, as she was on her way to perform the Vanishing spell that was supposed to scatter the lost children throughout the realm (someone else had done it for her, though she cannot fathom who. It could not have been Hazel; her magic was not as strong as that of the

Enchantress). The old woman gifted her with a greater measure of magic, the kind that the Enchantress thought had no limits. But she has been using this greater magic for more than three weeks now, and she can feel its toll, how it depletes her energy and steals her sleep, which further depletes her energy.

She uses this magic to propel them forward; otherwise it would take months to travel across the lands, since the looking ball prefers showing them one child at a time, and they must constantly backtrack (another of her annoyances; why not show all the children who vanished to Lincastle so that she and the Huntsman can save time and travel?).

The black mood, at its heart, is a result of feeling out of control. The Enchantress prefers feeling in control, and this magical looking ball erases that. She would like not to rely on it, but what else can she do?

An egg. How ridiculous.

She does not want an egg! She wants a child!

"So…supper?"

She has forgotten to answer the Huntsman. "Yes, that would be lovely." Her stomach has emptied out since lunch, though eating much of anything has been difficult.

He leaves her alone in the clearing where they have been resting for two days. The looking ball says the egg is here in these woods. They have not yet attempted to find it.

Because it is ridiculous.

The clearing has grown darker by the time the Huntsman reappears with a squirrel (which the Enchantress will not eat; she only eats greens and some of the nuts she finds in the forest) and a bowl of fresh greens with some seeds sprinkled on top.

"I found a patch of sunflowers," he says. He looks decidedly pleased with himself.

She tries to give him a smile, but she is not sure she succeeds.

Poor Huntsman. It is not his fault.

They eat in silence for a time. When she has almost finished her bowl the Enchantress glances at the Huntsman. His face is shadowed, his eyebrows drawn low over his eyes.

"Thinking your dark thoughts, Huntsman?" she says. She tries to make the words light, playful, but, once again, she is not sure she succeeds. They feel thick and heavy in her mouth.

The Huntsman looks up at her, startled from wherever he went in his mind. He shakes his head. "Only thinking of some I left behind."

"You do not talk much of these people."

She does not talk much about the people she left behind, either. It is safer that way. But she is curious about the the Huntsman's sadness. Did he leave behind a woman?

"Missing is a difficult emotion," the Huntsman says.

"Do you miss…" She cannot finish. Her heart gives a wrenching twist. She looks at the ground so he cannot see her eyes, but she feels her cheeks burn.

She cannot fall in love with the Huntsman. It would be another ridiculous notch in the ridiculous ladder she is climbing.

It is only that she sees *him* when she looks at the Huntsman.

The Huntsman stirs some leaves and piles together some branches. He rubs two twigs together and blows. A spark begins. The Enchantress helps it ignite.

He waits until the fire is settled before saying, "I left behind a mother, a father, and a sister," he says. "And friends who meant something."

The Enchantress nods, trying to swallow the thickness in her throat. She will have to protect this perimeter soon. She glances back at the white mare and the cart she pulls. The birds are quiet now, hopefully sleeping. The worst thing about changing children into blackbirds is that the blackbirds rarely stop tweeting.

The Huntsman settles on his haunches, stretching his legs out in front of him. He leans back on his elbows. "Has the ball shown anything different?" he says.

"I have not checked it this evening," she says.

He nods. "Should we check it now?"

She knows he is saying they should. She takes the ball out of her left shoe and wriggles her fingers. It grows to its normal size, from the size of a tiny speck of dust.

The ball glows to life, and the only thing in it, of course, is an egg.

The same egg.

The ridiculous egg.

The Enchantress sighs. The Huntsman sits up and peers closely.

"I think it is a dragon's egg," he says. He turns to the Enchantress. "Do dragons live in this land?"

The Enchantress knows nothing about dragons. Her mother did not care for them, so she never did, either. So she says, "I do not know."

"Hmm." The Huntsman squints his eyes as though he is looking through the woods. "I cannot imagine that a dragon's egg would be anything but dangerous."

"But if a child is inside of it..." How ridiculous it sounds. Vanishing spells do not put people in eggs. She has never heard of such a thing.

But a memory creeps from its hiding place. She Vanished once, and she was held in a suspended state for a time. She did not immediately become the Enchantress. She had been trapped in something similar to an egg. Something through which she could see, though her vision was distorted and hazy.

Well, it was not an egg. That would be—

"How will you turn whatever—whoever—is in an egg into a blackbird?" the Huntsman says. There is the trace of laughter in his voice.

She has wondered the same. Does she wait for the egg to hatch, or does she execute the Transformation spell as soon as they possess the egg?

The egg.

The Enchantress feels the black mood returning. She shoves it away.

The Huntsman begins to laugh. And she finds that it is contagious; she begins to laugh as well. They laugh and laugh and laugh until their stomachs hurt and their eyes are wet and their throats are hoarse.

"Oh, dear," the Enchantress says when they are finished. It feels so good to laugh for once.

The Huntsman shakes his head. "An egg," he says, and he chuckles again. "Can you imagine what the child inside it is thinking?"

The Enchantress shakes her head, too, and laughs again. "No," she says.

They laugh silently for a time before the Huntsman says, "Well. I suppose we should get some rest."

They should. But the Enchantress is not quite ready for this magical evening to be done. Still, she rises. "We will search for the egg in the morning?" It is the first time she has phrased the words as a question.

The Huntsman nods. "Perhaps more will be revealed tomorrow," he says. And then a hitch of laughter. "An egg."

The Enchantress presses her hand to her mouth to stifle her giggle. She turns and one leg buckles. The Huntsman is by her side in a moment.

"Careful," he says in her ear. "You are weary."

"It is the magic," she says.

"Perhaps we should wait a few days, then. Let you rest. Gain back your strength."

"I would like to be done with this," the Enchantress says.

"Yes," the Huntsman says. "But not at the risk of your life."

The Enchantress turns to him, gazing up into those blue eyes that feel so familiar. "Do we not all risk our lives for that which we believe in?" she says. It is not a noble thing, what she is doing. Not any nobler than others have done.

"And what do you believe in?" he says. His voice is soft, measured, a gentle wind across her face.

She drops her eyes and shakes her head. She does not know. She cannot tell him this.

He says, "I could help you," but before she can ask him what he means, he drops her hands as though they are flaming coals and hisses, "Creature. Get behind me."

So a creature has broken her defenses. She is more weary than she knew.

The creature, strangely, is not facing them, so they cannot see what kind it is. It is facing the opposite direction, as though looking deeper into the woods, as though it has not seen them at all. It is large and hulking, like a bison or a bear on four feet. The Huntsman says, "Stand back," and draws a dagger from his boot.

But before he can fling it, before it can twist through the air end over end over end, before it can lodge into the back of the creature's neck, a sound explodes from the rear end of the creature, vibrating the entire earth so violently that the Enchantress and the Huntsman stumble from left to right and back to front. The Huntsman releases his dagger. Noxious fumes follow the explosion in a giant, puffing cloud. The Enchantress and the

Huntsman watch the gray cloud, billowing toward them in slow motion, their mouths agape. The Huntsman's dagger slices through it, but the cloud barrels on. It hits the Huntsman first. He crumples, his feet folded beneath him, and before the Enchantress can think what to do, she, too, crumples.

The creature crashes off through the woods. The Huntsman's dagger lodges in a tree, right where the creature stood.

Cook stirs the soup. Potato soup was always the king's favorite, with a dusting of herbs and spices and soaked in the broth of chicken she has labeled in jars lining a shelf in the root cellar. Calvin did well with her instructions; even the root cellar door was closed behind him (Calvin has, historically, been terrible about closing doors and extinguishing torches).

She wonders, as she stirs, if Calvin knows that the eastern wall of the root cellar stops where the western wall of the dungeons begins. They do not lead to each other, of course, since that design might have given the prisoners, back when prisoners were kept in the regular dungeons of Fairendale castle, an easy escape and hiding place. In the ancient days, those charged with feeding the prisoners often commented that it would have been a worthwhile arrangement, however; it would have saved them the time of walking all the way across to the other side of the castle and braving the treacherous winding stairs. Cook only knew this because she had read every history book in Fairendale castle. She enjoyed history, and in every history someone had complained about this flaw in design.

When cooks from history ventured down into the root cellar, they could often hear prisoners talking to one another (Cook had read this as well). It must have been an eerie thing, as though the foods stored in jars—pickles and tomatoes and all sorts of jams—and the salted meat could talk. Were they mournful? Sprightly? Full of fury and wrath?

Cook has never heard those voices, since the dungeons were never necessary during King Sebastien's reign. He had simply killed those who deserved the dungeons. And now, the children rounded up by King Willis in a foolish attempt to eradicate magic—Cook still seethes at this appalling plan—are kept in the secret dungeons beneath the dungeons, which have no location on the castle maps. Only Calvin knows where they sit; he is the only one who can see and enter the door that leads to them.

These secret dungeons beneath the dungeons do not have typical doors on the cells but ones that require a magical key to open them. No one knows where the key is. No one knows, either, how many secret dungeons beneath the dungeons there are.

"Why are you cooking for the monster?" Calvin entered the kitchen silently while Cook was stirring the soup. She tries not to show how startled she is. She tries not to notice how angry he sounds.

But when Cook looks over her shoulder at the boy, she can see that his eyes hold all sorts of accusations. She watches them launch toward her, but before she can feel their piercing, she turns away.

"She wants to lure King Willis out of his room so that she can make his heart crooked again," Calvin says.

Cook smiles at the wall. Though he is not always smart in the kitchen, she loves Calvin's spirit.

She stops herself. She cannot love a boy. She was not made to love a boy. She cannot be a mother, she will never be a mother. Love is too dangerous, too unpredictable, too fallible. Love is something you can destroy, something that can destroy you, something that can be lost, and she has known too much of that already.

Her heart hollows itself out for a moment, wringing

and twisting and convulsing. And then it seems to absorb all the heat from the pot of soup she is stirring; it throbs and thrashes and blazes.

It says, *And yet you do.*

I do what? she says right back.

You do love him.

I do not.

"She is an evil monster." Calvin is unaware of Cook's inner battle, and he is not finished yet. "Why are you helping her with her plans?"

Cook turns around slowly. She chooses her words as though they are glass. "There are things that you cannot see, Calvin," she says. "You are only a child." She says the words gently, but she can feel the fire in her eyes.

"I know more than you think," Calvin says. His eyes hold fire, too. "Remember? You left me here to fend for myself." His hands ball up into fists, hanging at his thighs. He finishes with, "I know more than you think." The last words are delivered with a higher, reedier voice, as though they contain every emotion it is possible for a human to feel—but mostly anger, disappointment, fear. Cook works hard to keep her eyes dry. She works hard to remain in place, beside the soup, at a distance that does not speak of love.

But oh, her boy. She would like to take him in her

arms and hold him while he cries. She would like to kiss the top of his messy hair and admit how glad she is to be back home. She would like to tell him that he is magnificent and lovely and delightful—and loved. He has only known tragedy and loss in his young life, and he deserves this proclamation of love and worth, does he not?

She almost moves. What holds her in place is the knowledge that there are things she must do in her future that Calvin will not understand. She will leave again; it is assured because of who she is. She will not break his heart, as it has been so cruelly broken in the past—in losing his parents in the eruption of a Fire Mountain; in being cast off by an aunt and uncle who could have raised him but chose, instead, to leave him to his fate; in coming here, to her gruff kitchen of the past.

There is so much she would like to say. But she snares the words, rolls them up, and presses them down to her depths, where all the shadows of past love reside.

It is better this way.

Cook takes a deep breath, and what she says, instead of all the other words that have turned over in her mind, is, "I have put an enchantment on this pot. Anything cooked in it will also hold the enchantment." They are whispered words, and she leaves it at that and turns back to her stirring.

Calvin is quiet for so long that Cook thinks he has left the room. But then he says, in a voice that would never be called a whisper, "What kind of enchantment have you put on it?"

Cook whirls around and raises a finger to her lips. "She must not know," she says. Her voice is fiercer now, and she can see the immediate effect it has on the boy. He was not expecting it; she is sorry.

But of course she does not say so. She has always played the part of the stern authoritarian in this kitchen. It is what the boy needs, to be shown that he is capable of doing what he needs to do.

Or so she tells herself.

Her next words are even softer than her previous ones. "An enchantment to resist all other enchantments. One that will protect the king from dark magic of ill intent." She has never actually attempted this spell before. King Willis will be an experiment. She does not know why she did not think of the spell before now; she might have saved King Willis from the throne's influence and the entire village of Fairendale from the tragedy of losing its children. It is another notch of regret in a long line of them.

She can only say that she did not know about the

spell before, and, somehow, this afternoon, it presented itself in her mind, as though it had always been there. She conducted it and promptly fell asleep on the kitchen floor for several hours. It was a powerful, complicated spell, an intricate balance of dark and light magic.

Good thing she gave Calvin something to occupy himself this afternoon, or he might have stumbled upon her, sleeping.

Calvin stares at her. A smile spreads across his face in slow motion. It falters a little when he says, "You have the gift of magic." It is not a question. She knows he has known for a while, but now she has confirmed it.

Cook does not answer. Instead, she turns back to the soup, and when next she looks behind her, Calvin is gone. But a note is pinned to the door. She crosses the room and retrieves it.

"Perhaps you could prepare a little more for the prophets and the children in the dungeons beneath the dungeons. Love, Calvin." His handwriting is atrocious, but Cook clasps the note to her chest and closes her eyes.

Love, Calvin.

Yes. She does.

Cook crosses the kitchen to begin another pot of soup. There is plenty of food to go around, now that her magic has coaxed the garden back into its flourishing state. This pot will not be magical, but the bowls that hold what is cooked inside it will be, in a completely different and miraculous way.

She tries her best to still her thoughts and dampen the stirrings in her heart.

Love is a dangerous thing.

Truths

Matilda spent months that turned into years trying to learn more about the prophet Bregdon, trying to find him, trying to ensure that the magical items she had made remained hidden. Her daughter turned six and then seven, and the prophet did not come (nor did her husband, but Matilda had already reconciled that possibility). Matilda was consumed with a desperate need to know whether she had done something good or something entirely awful.

It was a breathless need that curled up inside her and swelled to nearly unbearable proportions.

She searched every book she owned. Bregdon had once been a prophet of White Wind. But he had disappeared many years ago, and, with him, all record of his whereabouts.

One day she came into possession of an ancient tome about the prophets of White Wind, buried beneath a pile of old texts in the village bookshop.

Bredgon, the volume said, had died before she was born.

She looked at the prophet in the picture. With the exception of his crooked, yellow teeth (the prophet who had visited her had gleaming white ones—still crooked, though), he was surely the same man.

It was impossible. Matilda had not been visited by a spirit. But there it was, printed on the pages. His birth date and his death date. There was his picture—his cloudy head, his catching smile, those strange eyes. She sat staring at it for a very long time.

He had not been a spirit. Or had he? Could this explain why he had been able to carry a heavy throne like it was nothing at all? Could it explain his sudden disappearances and reappearances? Could it explain his pale skin and the celestial glow that followed him?

There was no celestial glow. She was being ridiculous.

Matilda closed the book and returned it to the bookseller, who rewarded her with a sour look, likely hoping that she would purchase the book. It was much too expensive for Matilda. She was a Healer, and Healers were not paid very well. She was paid, more often than she would like, with chickens and pastries and loaves of homemade bread, rather than money.

It was something, though. If people wanted to pay her with a week of suppers, who was she to turn them away? She would not have to cook for her daughter, which freed up her time for…what? Searching for Bregdon? The search had overtaken practically everything.

Aleen was in the cottage when Matilda returned home. "I must go for a walk, gather some wild herbs," Matilda told her daughter. She kissed Aleen on the top of her forehead and smoothed down her wild hair. Aleen could never be persuaded to brush her hair, and it often looked as though snakes lived in it. When she had time, Matilda tried to tame it. But it was a lost cause.

Matilda slipped out the door before her daughter could ask any questions.

She checked behind her a dozen times or more to make sure Aleen did not follow her into the woods; she did not want her daughter to see what she had come here to do. She had a great many questions to ask Bregdon, and she intended to Summon him.

She called his name—the full one he had given her during one of his visits. It bounced around the trees and came back to meet her. She tried again, this time with her staff in hand. Once again, the name bounced around the trees and came back to meet her. She placed the staff on the ground, drew herself up to her full height, and spoke the name once more, in the most commanding voice she could manage.

A flash exploded in front of her. The prophet looked stricken, unmoored for a moment. She expected him to be a bit angry, but this was not the case. His eyes fastened on her face. "You Summoned me," he said, and the wrinkled smile sank into her. Her guilt dissolved.

"I wondered if you gave me the correct name," she said.

He lifted his chin. "I would not have lied."

"But you hide."

Something flickered across Bregdon's face. "People are not so welcoming of a man who is supposed to be dead."

"Why are you not dead?" Matilda said.

Bregdon shook his head. "I do not know. I only know that I am alive."

"Are you?" Matilda narrowed her eyes. He did look alive, she had to admit, but she knew that illusions could often be deceiving and difficult to spot. She had been tricked by several of them in her past, and she did not want to be tricked again.

"No," Bregdon said. "But do not ask me to explain. I cannot, even if I wanted to."

They were quiet for some minutes.

"You want something with me," Bregdon said at last. It was not a question.

"I want to know who you are," she said.

"You know who I am. It is how you Summoned me."

"I do not know anything about you except your name." He could not argue with her, and she saw the defeat settle across his face. He was hers until she permitted him to leave. She could keep him here all day, all month, all year if she liked. It is the way of a Summoning spell. One must be dismissed from it.

She felt powerful, for once in her life.

Bregdon let out a long breath. He told her about his life of struggle with another prophet who craved power and notoriety and superiority—to be the best prophet in the land. He told her the prophet wanted him dead, and, to save his own life, Bregdon had faked death and disappeared—exiled himself far into the uncharted northern lands so that the two could continue to coexist in the world. He had woken one day back in White Wind, his original home. He had searched for the other prophet for a time, though the only way his self-inflicted Exile spell could have been broken was by the prophet's death.

"Who was the other prophet?" Matilda said. She wanted to know everything. Her curiosity was a hungry thing.

Bregdon waved his hand. "It matters not who he was. What matters is that I am here, and I have been given a directive."

"By whom?"

"It is impossible to say."

"And you do not question it?" Matilda found this strange. She questioned everything.

"No," Bregdon said. "I have never had cause to question why I am told to do what I do. I simply do it."

"But who is running your directive? Would you not rather be a master of yourself?" Matilda blinked, unable to comprehend the submission of such a powerful prophet.

"I *am* the master of myself," Bregdon said. This time his voice was clipped, as though it held a smidge of anger.

"But you said yourself that you do not know where the Visions come from or who has given them."

"Do you know the voice inside you that directs what you do?" Bregdon said.

"It is my own," Matilda said.

"Precisely," Bregdon said, and he left it at that.

"These items," Matilda said. She collected her thoughts, examined them briefly, and chose one. "Have they caused harm since they were created?"

"They remain hidden," Bregdon said. "For another time, long from this one."

It did not make her feel better.

"How can you know for sure that they are needed?" Matilda said.

"I am a prophet," Bregdon said. "All prophets know such things. But I am more powerful than most." He did not say the words as though he was proud of them. In fact, they appeared to make him exceedingly sad. "I have been alive for a very long time."

So this was the source of his sadness. She could see it in his eyes.

Matilda stifled the urge to touch him. He had not told her everything, and that angered her.

But then, as though he sensed her wavering, he wove around her a fantastical story of many lives lived and left and lived again, stronger.

"You have lived more than one life?" She could not hide her skepticism. Matilda was not a woman given to fancy and frivolity.

"I have," Bregdon said. The corners of his lips

turned up a little, as though he was amused by her skepticism. "I have lived more lives than most are permitted."

"And you come back to life. Stronger than you were before." It sounded too incredible to be true. It broke every rule she knew.

"Yes," Bregdon said. "Every time I live again, I am permitted to gift someone with something before I die." He paused. "And I believe it is time to gift you."

Matilda looked at him, her heart pounding. She had no need of his gifts. But what she said, instead, was, "I would not take your life. It is not in my nature to do so."

"It makes no matter to me," Bregdon said. "I will simply come back again." He sounded very tired. Tired of his many lives? Matilda wondered what she would do with so many lives.

They were quiet for some minutes before Bregdon said, "I could grant you life like mine," but the way he said it made her think he would never wish his life on anyone. A hollow ache began in her chest.

"I do not want to live forever," Matilda said. She thought about all the people she would have to watch die, and she knew she spoke the truth. She did not want to live forever. She only wanted the one more chance she would get with the magical cauldron, as Bregdon had foretold.

Bregdon loosened a long breath. "Nor would I," he said, and that was all.

Matilda thought of her daughter, back at the cottage. "Perhaps you could spare a supernatural protection for my daughter."

Bregdon's eyes crinkled. "It has already been done."

Matilda felt the gladness warm her chest. "And magic?"

"She has it in abundance. She will begin accidentally showing the signs soon."

Matilda nodded. There was nothing else she could ask. She had everything she needed.

Except for knowledge. So she said, "I would like the gift of knowing where each of these objects I have made are hidden at all times."

There was only the slightest pause before Bregdon said, "Yes. Very well."

The prophet then touched her, and once she felt the burning magic pierce her skin, unroll itself, and blast through her limbs, the prophet fell down in a lifeless heap.

Because Matilda did not know whether this was his last life, she laid the prophet in the crypt on the outskirts of town, where the paupers were laid to rest. She did it in the dark of night, as was the custom of the people of White Wind. They did not need bodies for funerals; only an object representing the dead one's life.

There would be no funeral for Bregdon.

Matilda tended the body during the days that followed. And on the fourth day, he was no longer in the crypt.

Resolutions

He wakes with a jolt.

He is blind.

Oh, he is blind!

Everywhere Yerin looks, it is black. It is not the blackness of the dungeons beneath the dungeons. It is the blackness of being blind.

He cries out.

"What is it, Grandpapa?" Someone touches his arm. He knows these gentle hands. They belong to Agnes, one of the children from Fairendale, who is, herself, blind. She is the daughter of Sir Merrick, the second-in-command of the king's guard, who died (though she does not know it yet) on the dust of the dragon lands of Morad.

Yerin feels quite foolish admitting his fear to her, but

perhaps she, of all people, will understand.

"My eyes," he says. His voice comes out as hardly more than a whisper. "I cannot see."

He has heard stories of prophets whose Sight was taken from them. Sometimes it happened because the prophet was nearing his or her one hundred forty-third birthday, the day and evening when a prophet is permitted to use magic one more time to achieve something great and magnificent—followed by their immediate death. A sacrificial act. Aleen—the woman he loved, who was imprisoned with him for a time in these very dungeons—had chosen the way of the One Last Great Act. He misses her every day.

He does not know what she did. He does not know if it accomplished what she wanted it to accomplish. He does not know if her sacrifice meant anything at all.

A prophet is not permitted to know such things.

How is he supposed to choose his One Last Great Act without his sight? Without his greater Sight that enables him—or enabled him, up until recently—to See the future? He cannot even see what is in front of him now.

Yerin shakes his head.

"What is wrong with your eyes?" Agnes says. She touches his lids.

"I am blind." Yerin cannot help the fear and anguish

that enrobe his words, that carry them to the walls, where they collide and break.

Aleen had not gone blind in the days leading up to her act. But every prophet's journey is different, and there is no guarantee for anyone.

At least he is in good company with the blind, here in these dungeons. There is not only Agnes but the three blind mice as well.

"Are you sure you are blind, or is it simply dark in here?" Agnes says.

It is a very dark dungeon. Most of the children, in the beginning, tried to keep their eyes closed, so absolute was the darkness. But the boy from upstairs—Calvin—has kept them supplied with candles, and the mice bring them when they can. It is not always dark anymore.

And, too, there is the glow of the bones in the cell beside this one. Yerin cannot watch and observe it now. The thought makes him shiver. Not that he could do anything about it in the first place, but the knowing is better than not knowing.

Agnes lifts the back of her hand to Yerin's forehead. "Do you have a fever, perhaps?" she says. He knows he does not. Even though he feels weak, he does not feel feverish. Yerin takes the girl's hand. He has grown to love her as a grandfather might in the days they have spent locked away. She is optimistic and hopeful, and he longs to feel that optimism and hope, to make it his own.

Perhaps she senses this need; she says, "It is not so terrible being blind. You will see through your other senses. Your ears, your hands, your nose."

Yerin nods.

"Calvin is coming," says one of the children, and Yerin is hit, anew, with the disappointing and terrifying knowledge that his sight is gone; he really can see nothing. He swallows hard.

"Others become your eyes, too," Agnes whispers.

"Hello," Calvin says. His voice sounds chipper, empty of its usual solemnity. The smell of soup stirs a rumble in Yerin's belly. "I have brought a very large pot of soup." Yerin can hear the boy set the pot on the stone ground, and it does, indeed, sound like a very large pot.

"How did you get this pot of soup down the stairs?" Yerin says.

He can hear the smile in Calvin's voice when he says, "Magic."

"You have the gift of magic?" Agnes says.

"No," Calvin says. "But Cook does."

"Cook?" Yerin says. He tries to call up her face in his mind, but he has met so many in the years he has been alive; his mind does not cooperate.

"She made the soup and enchanted it," Calvin says.

"Will it hurt us?" a child says.

"No," Calvin says, and Yerin can hear the grin in his voice again. Has Calvin ever been so happy? And then the boy says the words he must have been waiting to say: "It will never run out." He delivers this last bit with so much glee stuffed inside it that Yerin cannot help but smile, too.

The children murmur around him. Yerin hears the splash of liquid and assumes Calvin is dishing some soup into bowls. Someone shoves a bowl into Yerin's hand. It is hot and heavy. He fumbles for the spoon.

"Yerin," Calvin says. "Are you well?" The splashing of soup continues.

"He woke up blind," Agnes says.

No one says anything for a time.

Calvin is the one who breaks the silence. His voice wobbles when he says, "Why?"

It is the one word with which Yerin has been wrestling as well.

"We do not know," he says. He tries to make his voice strong, confident.

"And your Prophet's Sight?" Calvin says.

"Still a bit blurry," Yerin says. A half-truth. No sense in alarming the children.

Another bowl scratches against the stone floor. Calvin is silent for a few minutes before he says, "The other prophets—are they alive or dead?"

"Still sleeping," Agnes says. It is the hope of every child here. Sleeping, not dead.

The dungeons are filled with the clanking of spoons against bowls and the slurping of soup. Yerin dips into his bowl, lets the hot liquid warm his throat. The soup is a kaleidoscope of flavor; he never knew food could have a color, but this one is all of them, bursting into the darkness.

The only sounds in the dungeons are eating ones, but Yerin can still feel Calvin's presence, pressed up against the bars. After a time, the boy says, "Your bowls will become clean as soon as you are finished eating. And you will be able to use them again. The soup will fill your bowls whenever you desire it, now that it has touched your bowls."

"Extraordinary," Yerin says. "And this was done by the magic of Cook?"

"Yes," Calvin says. "She is a powerful sorceress." Yerin can hear the pride in the boy's voice, as though Cook might belong to him, or he to her.

A powerful sorceress is not always a good thing. Yerin examines his gut, which usually alerts him to danger. He feels nothing, but he cannot be certain this means Cook is no danger or he has simply lost all of his connections with the gift of prophecy.

"She also made this candle," Calvin says. Yerin cannot see it, but he assumes the boy holds up a candle. "It will never stop burning." A rattle sounds, as though Calvin has shoved the candle through the bars. "And some blankets that warm when you feel cold." A shuffling. "And she has woven a spell to protect the king from the monster."

Yerin sits up straight. The monster. He forgot the monster in his shock and grief at waking up blind. "The monster is still here?" he says.

"Yes. She is strange, though. She does not seem like she came to hurt anyone." Calvin's voice sounds unsure. "But Cook enchanted the king's soup so he is protected from any dark magic that may exist in the castle." The boy pauses for a moment and then adds, "Dark magic of ill intent. I believe that is what she said."

Yerin nods. "Good," he says. He can hear the sounds of Calvin preparing to leave. He says, "Calvin. Can you see the bones in the corner of the other cell, the bones we have been watching?"

"Yes," Calvin says.

"And what do they look like now?"

Calvin hesitates. "They look as though they are arranging themselves into the map of a person," he says at last. "And they are glowing much brighter."

The air seems to suck right out of the dungeons for a minute. Yerin tries to clear the heaviness from his throat. "Thank you, Calvin. For what you have given us."

"I will still check on you," Calvin says. "And I continue working to free you."

Yerin knows, with sudden certainty, that this freedom will not happen before he dies, but he says, "Thank you. Your courage is remarkable. I hope you always know what you mean to us and to the castle and to the greater world."

"I am just an ordinary boy," Calvin says.

"No," Yerin says. He slides his hand between the bars of the cage. Calvin's cold hand meets his. "You are extraordinary."

The only sound in the dungeons beneath the dungeons are the boy's steps retreating and the children still slurping their soup.

And despite everything—the captivity, the blindness, the bones that are moving—Yerin feels glad.

Cora stands in an underground room, one of two in the secret passageway beneath the fountains of Fairendale village. This is not the main one; it is much smaller and slightly colder. Only one torch burns above her head.

Today she has brought the prince—the prince she transformed into a blackbird, the prince she cannot, now, return to his former state because her magical powers seem to have left her—into this small, secluded room. Long ago she enchanted the door so that no one but her can enter. A matter of precaution. As is her decision to now keep the prince—as a blackbird—in this small closet. This game has become dangerous now that Sir Greyson knows her secrets.

Well, not all her secrets. She recounts the rest to the blackbird.

This is what happens when one has no companions. It is true she has Grimm; she could tell him her secrets, but he is a cat, an animal. At least she knows the blackbird is a boy.

Does he retain his humanlike ability to process speech? This she does not know.

It feels good to unburden herself. She starts with, "I have become a dragon rider." The words swell in the small room, until they feel as though they might suffocate her. She never wanted to be a dragon rider. But it was not in her power to be anything else. She touched a dragon; she felt the spark. Now she is a rider. Now she is bound to this dragon she does not even like—may even despise. She must figure out how to be free of him.

And, in fact, that is what she plans to do next. It is a small detour, perhaps, but a necessary one. She is afraid that becoming a rider has also stolen her magical powers. And these she needs much more than she needs a young, impulsive, highly annoying dragon.

"I will take you to the dragon," Cora says. The blackbird flutters his wings. Cora pats his back. "I will not let the dragon hurt you. He is bound to me; if I do not want him to hurt you, there is nothing to fear."

She is not entirely sure this is true; the dragon has, after all, wounded her. She has not seen him to confirm that he, too, is wounded in the very same place.

But she has a plan. Cora always has a plan. The dragon will not listen to anything she has to say until he sees the prince. She will show him the prince as a blackbird, and then she will release the bird and hope he finds his way back here.

Something clatters in the larger room, as though someone has entered. Cora opens the door a crack and peers through it. Sir Greyson stares at her with his madly beautiful blue eyes. She slams the door in his face. He cannot open it. She will not allow it.

"Did you follow me?" Her words are tight and angry, though she feels more sadness than anything else.

She thought they were done with the following. She told him she did not need him. She thought he took it to heart.

But he is outside the door, leaning against it. She can feel his warmth—no, she cannot. Her mind—her heart, more specifically—is playing a trick on her. She presses a hand to her chest and says, "Go away."

"No," he says. He sounds resolute, unmoving, unlike the last time they argued.

"Why are you here?" she says. She tries to wrap the words in anger, but they come out sounding like a puff of smoke, like she is burned up within her anger and the only thing left is loneliness. She straightens her shoulders. The bird flutters his wings.

"I have come to talk you out of what you plan to do," Sir Greyson says.

There. Now she feels the anger. She says, "You have been at the castle. You smell of betrayal."

Sir Greyson opens the door of the small room. Cora gasps. The door is not supposed to let anyone in but her.

Now there are two of them, trapped in this small

room. She tries to push past him, but he catches her arms and draws her close.

"You are wounded," he says.

How does he know?

"I can feel it." He presses a hand to his chest.

Her chest clenches.

"Where?" he says.

"It is none of your concern," she says, trying to keep her voice steady.

His eyes turn soft. "Cora," he says. "Please."

She does not say anything.

He says, "It is the wound of a dragon." He stares at her, his eyes unblinking. He is trying to read her, take her apart, confirm the gravity of this injury. She will not let him have anything. She carefully arranges her face into an expression of distaste and shakes him off.

The bird twitters. Sir Greyson looks at him. "So this is the prince."

She does not answer.

They are both quiet for some time. And then Sir Greyson fixes his eyes on her and says, once more, "Cora," and the way it curves around her, the way it pulls her back to the moment, the way it vibrates in her heart, almost cracks her.

Almost.

She opens her mouth to say something, but Sir Greyson holds up a hand and says, "Please. Hear me out."

She supposes she can at least give him this.

"The king and queen are fleeing the castle." His eyes are wide when he says it. Cora cannot help her own eyes widening in surprise.

"Why?" The word comes out harsh, accusatory.

Sir Greyson sighs. "There has been a new development," he says. "A monster now sits on the throne of Fairendale."

"A monster has sat on the throne of Fairendale since the days of King Sebastien," Cora says.

Sir Greyson tilts his head and looks at her for a long moment before saying, "This monster looks like she was raised from the dead."

"She?" Cora crosses her arms across her chest. Why do monsters have to be female?

Sir Greyson shrugs. "She looks like a woman. Like a dead woman." He waves a hand. "I cannot explain it. But I believe we may all have to flee. She is dangerous, that much is certain."

"Fairendale is my home," Cora says, as though the matter is settled.

"Fairendale is not a home for anyone any longer," Sir

Greyson says.

"The people will not leave, not until they have their children." Cora lifts her chin. Let him counter that one.

"That is what I fear as well," he says, and his eyes drop to the ground. Silence balloons around them.

At long last, Sir Greyson speaks: "Perhaps we can all hide out in the secret passageway."

Cora shakes her head. "Hiding is a coward's way." At Sir Greyson's stricken look, she adds, "There is not enough food to sustain us here. We have used most of the provisions." The room in which they are standing, in fact, used to be where the provisions were stored. Now there are only a few jars of jam lining the shelves.

Sir Greyson eyes the cabinets, and she can tell that he knows what she says is true. She does not like the defeated look on his face, though she cannot say why; he is nothing to her anymore. She says, "We will figure something out."

"Perhaps your magic," he says. "It saved the village once, did it not?"

Cora does not answer. She cannot bear to tell him that her magical powers have disappeared.

Sir Greyson looks at the bird. "I will take the king and queen somewhere safe. And then I will come back for all of you."

The dagger in her chest twists, an agonizing move. So he will be leaving her after all. No matter. As she said before, she does not need him.

"And where will you go?" The words are much more difficult to shove out of her mouth than she would have expected.

Sir Greyson studies his boots, which have a hole in the right shoe. "I do not know."

"Then do not go." Cora presses a hand against her mouth. Take the words back. She would like to. But they are between them, betraying her. Sir Greyson looks at her with eyes so tortured that she must blink fast as she turns her face to the blackbird. To the prince. To the son of the king and queen.

They are silent for a very long time. Even the blackbird remains still. Cora lets the memories of all the years flash over her, the years of waiting for Sir Greyson, the years of settling for another, the years with her daughter, after her husband was lost at sea.

"Did you want to be a queen?" Sir Greyson's voice startles her from her thoughts, and the words feel like a dangerous fire. "Is that what this is all about? You are glad the king and queen are leaving so that you can take the throne?"

Cora's anger ignites. How dare he. How dare he

assign such motives as these. She would not take the throne of Fairendale if it were handed to her.

Would she?

"Why else did you retain your magical abilities if not to be a queen?" Sir Greyson's eyes are glassy.

"I did not ask to remain a sorceress," Cora replies evenly. She tries to control the anger flaming in her throat. "I did not ask for any of it." She says the words with such intensity—controlling the anger clearly did not work this time—that the ground beneath their feet shakes. The torches flicker. Sir Greyson touches a wall. His eyes, when he lifts them from his hand to her face, are full of fear.

He is afraid of her.

This knowing does not bring her pleasure.

"But royalty is what you always wanted," Sir Greyson says.

Cora feels a wrenching sob climb into her throat. She swallows it.

The man she loved so much never knew the true motivations of her heart. But she was never completely his. And he was never completely hers. He also belonged to the kingdom. He was a king's man.

Cora says, "I never wanted a throne. I only wanted a life."

"But you had a life. With me."

"We never had a chance," Cora says. She wants to hurt him the way he has hurt her. "A king always stood in our way." She throws the final dagger: "A king was always more important to you than I could ever be."

Sir Greyson shakes his head. "No," he says. His eyes plead with her to understand, but she will never understand. She was supposed to marry him. He was supposed to love her. And instead he left her to be a captain. "If you would just try to understand."

"There is nothing to understand," Cora says. "There is something fundamentally different about you and me. We could never be anything more than we have already been. Two passing ships, setting sail in opposite directions."

Sir Greyson stares at her for a minute, his mouth dropped open slightly. Then he shakes his head, turns on his heel, and walks away from her.

Likely for the last time.

The king does not come.

Yasmin waits inside the dining hall, the large table empty of people but filled with food. There are sweet rolls and pies, roasted lamb and potatoes swimming in butter, fresh greens slathered in oil. Yasmin breathes in the delightful scent of nourishment and feels the ever-present pinch of her pleasureless condition.

What she would give to taste this food.

Her annoyance at having been stood up is slight—at least until it is half past the dining hour and the food is in danger of growing too cold. The serving boy moves into the room, presumably to refill water or clear away plates. He looks confused that she is the only one in the room.

"The king," Yasmin says. She intentionally arranges her voice into a nonchalant growl. "He is in his chambers?"

The boy—she believes she heard the cook call him Calvin—looks at her for a moment before nodding his head. "It is where he has been…" He fumbles for a bit, then adds, "Madame."

A smart boy with a good sense for who holds power. She likes him already.

Yasmin rises with all the grace she possesses (which is quite a lot) and revels in the look of surprise that flashes across the boy's face as she moves past him, out the doors, and down the hall toward the bedchambers.

If the king will not come to her, she will go to him.

The hallway is lined with portraits of past kings. She

slows, examining them as she passes. There are several she does not recognize, but she does recognize her son. She presses a hand to his cheek. He looks much the same in the portrait as he did the last time she saw him pacing in the mirror (she has, for this day, at least, completely ignored his presence, though he is persistent in calling. She is not ready to speak with him, and she would rather he believe he is invisible than know she is deliberately disregarding him; she fears the latter could come back to haunt her.).

Yasmin moves on. She has a purpose: draw the king out, dine with him, use him however she sees fit.

Not a single person meets her along her way. They must all be hiding. What cowardly people. Yasmin clenches her jaw. They do not deserve a place in her kingdom; she wants only the brave and pure of heart.

Pure of heart? She stops and tilts her head, unsure where the thought originated. The Grim Reaper is not pure of heart. Her mind is a muddle. She must clear it.

She balls her fists and moves on.

It is a maze of hallways, but something guides her, something internal and instinctual. Perhaps she was meant to be a queen after all. Perhaps Sebastien was right.

The aroma of sweet rolls reaches her. Impossible. But

when she walks a bit farther, she sees the dining hall again. She turns around. She must have chosen the wrong hallway. She must have walked one large circle. Yasmin starts off in the other direction. She finds herself, this time, in the kitchen.

The boy is there, his hands raised in front of him as though surrendering. "Take me to the king," she says. All her annoyance and frustration tangle around the words, hooking barbs to their ends.

"Follow me, my lady," says the boy in a voice that sounds very much like a mouse. Yasmin smiles to herself. Perhaps fear is the way to obedience.

She tests her theory with another harsh commandment: "Bring some sweet rolls."

The boy nods, races into the dining hall, and bursts out with the large plate of piled pastries. Yasmin follows him down the same hallway she walked before. She sees the portraits, she sees her son, she sees the resting chairs in various colors and designs.

This time her walking ends at a door. Yasmin glances around. This portion of the castle is unfamiliar; she is sure it was not here before. She shakes her head, takes the plate of sweet rolls from the boy, and says, "Thank you," before remembering a queen does not need to thank a servant. The boy, however, rewards her with a look of astonishment and then a small smile before fleeing toward the hallway of portraits.

Yasmin watches him for a moment, after which she turns back to the king's door. She lifts her hand to knock, but before she can, the door is flung open, and another woman nearly upsets the sticky plate in her hurry to leave. There is a large jewel-covered bag in her hand. The king stands behind her, hauling a large trunk.

So they are leaving already, are they? Not anymore.

Yasmin looks at the bag and the trunk, then lifts her eyes to the king. His are large, brown, misty. His mouth gapes open.

"Hello," Yasmin says.

The woman, who must be the queen, gasps. Yasmin basks in her horror.

"Were you going somewhere?" Yasmin says.

The queen straightens. She has lovely golden hair that falls around her shoulders in gentle waves. Her skin is smooth and unlined, and the crown on her head sparkles in the flickering torchlight from the hall. Yasmin straightens as well. She is taller than the queen, though not by much.

This is news. She was taller when she first came. Is she shrinking? Yasmin takes a moment to glance at her feet, where her dress has begun to bunch. She must be shrinking, then.

She tries to ignore the icy stone that drops into her chest.

Neither the king nor the queen speaks, so Yasmin continues. "I came to ask you to supper," she says in the direction of the king. She hopes the queen will not think she is included in this invitation; she is not. Most definitely not.

Yasmin holds up the sweet rolls. The king's eyes flick to them and back to Yasmin. But his eyes are drawn back to the sweet rolls, as she knew they would be.

The queen turns to the king. "Willis," she says, and her voice holds a warning.

"It will not hurt to dine with her, will it?" King Willis says.

"I am here to help, not to hurt," Yasmin says. She smoothes her voice into a melodic song. She holds the plate closer to the king and queen. "You can trust me."

The queen shakes her head. "Willis," she says again, this time with a note of desperation.

The king's eyes hold the queen's gaze. They seem to be speaking without speaking—about her? Yasmin tries not to acknowledge the fire of rage that gusts into her throat; she will have the last say.

The king at last gives a small nod. "I will dine with

you," he says, and he drops the trunk, walks out the door, and heads toward the dining hall, as though he is the leader.

When the queen moves to follow him, Yasmin says, "I only have need of the king today. Perhaps in the near future the queen will join us? Tomorrow evening?"

King Willis turns and looks at his queen. She does not look at him, however; her eyes fix on Yasmin. Yasmin lifts her chin and stares back, the challenge sizzling between them. At last the queen nods. Do her shoulders slump? Yasmin thinks they might. Good.

She will break them both, king and queen.

"I will have them prepare you something," King Willis says. He moves toward the queen and wraps his hands around the tops of her arms. He leans to kiss her forehead. Yasmin turns her face away. "You will be in your bedchambers?" the king says.

The queen does not answer his question. She only says, "There is some reading I must do," and the king nods and spins on his heel, a graceful move for a man so large.

Yasmin almost tells him to kiss his queen one more time, since this is the last time he will see her for a while. But she presses her lips together and follows him—not too far behind; she still has the authority—to the dining hall, where they sit and eat and commiserate. King Willis is a brilliant man.

At half past eight, the king stands to go. "I am not yet done with you," Yasmin says, her voice pressed silky smooth. "First you must come sit on the throne. You are, after all, the king."

King Willis looks as though he would like nothing more than to flee; fear flashes clearly across his face. Yasmin stands and sends a smile in his direction. "Follow me, please," she says. She places her threat perfectly within the "please." The king obeys.

"Sit on the throne," she says when they have arrived at the platform within the throne room. King Willis stands instead, like a tree rooted to the earth.

No matter. Yasmin's first task for the Grim Reaper was rooting up trees. She shoves King Willis. He stumbles into the throne, and the throne glows violet.

Yasmin waits for a moment before saying, "You will sleep and eat in this throne room—on this throne, to be precise. You will not leave again."

Yasmin is satisfied when King Willis says, in a flat and emotionless voice: "Yes. I will."

And though she has accomplished what she set out to accomplish, Yasmin's laugh rings hollow and dry.

She feels absolutely nothing.

King Willis, however, is not caught in a web of Yasmin's making; he is entirely in control of his wits, thanks to the spell Cook wove over his meal and the sweet rolls as she prepared supper. This spell is much more potent than Yasmin's powers of persuasion.

When he agreed to sleep in the throne, King Willis thought it was all over for him. He witnessed the damage the throne could do to his will, the way it could bend him into someone completely different than who he knew himself to be. But he was surprised—and nearly giddy, to be honest—to learn that the throne has no more hold on him than fresh greens have on his dining pleasure.

At long last, he is free.

Not only that, but when he sat on the throne this time, a strange warmth surged into his body, the kind that lifts a spirit and permits it to fly. He saw the violet glow, but he felt the shift, as though evil was exchanged for good. And perhaps that is true; only time will tell.

King Willis believes he is changed. And so he must now don a mask.

He arranges his face carefully, empties it of all emotion and care. His eyes become impassive; they are the eyes of an automaton.

Let Yasmin think she has some power over him. She has none.

And while she is reveling in her power that is no power at all, he will discover her plans. Instead of fleeing, he will play the hero, for once in his life.

When Yasmin sends for the page—Garth; King Willis remembers his name—and commands him to bring a down pillow and a blanket for the king, who will sleep on the throne, and the boy returns with the requested items, King Willis is ready for him. He slips a small scrap of parchment to Garth. On it, he has written, "Do not worry, Clarion. I am well. The throne will not have me this time."

He is certain of it.

This time he will win.

Unravelings

In the next several months, Matilda periodically searched her mind to see where the objects she had created were hidden. They would visit her in a flash of light on the haze of a cloud. She would see the spinning wheel, still safety buried beneath the ground. She would see the cauldron somewhere in Guardia, in a cave guarded by a dragon with vivid blue eyes and the whitest scales she had ever seen, a blanket of snowflakes wrapping him. She would see the magical throne, hidden in the Weeping Woods, inside a small cottage. She never saw who lived in the cottage. She hoped it was Bregdon.

She did not know the purpose these items served, tucked away, but she did not want to unearth them and risk their capture by the wrong hands. So she let them lie.

At the end of that year, she saw the throne move to

Fairendale castle, and she wondered. She saw the king who sat on it, and he was kind-hearted and true and steadfast. She was glad.

Matilda died before she could witness the evil the throne would unleash inside that castle.

It was a fever that took her, one carried on a cold wind. She collapsed in the streets of White Wind, as though dignity were not permitted in death. She was vaguely aware of someone carrying her, roughly, to bed, some words from a Healer, and a man's gruff voice, raised in fury. She could not see, could not speak, could not comprehend.

She burned for two days. It was agonizing.

And then she was gone. She did not even get to kiss her daughter one more time.

Bregdon met her in death.

"I died," she said simply.

"You live again," he said.

"Like you?"

"Like me, but also unlike me."

Matilda did not understand this. Her head felt large and heavy. Of only one thing she could be certain. "I cannot feel the objects I have made," she said. "Nor can I see them."

"You must relinquish your hold on them," Bregdon

said. His voice was soft, gentle. "All of them. This is the only way you can become what the realm needs you to be."

Matilda sat up. She was in the crypt. Aleen must have carried her here. She must have laid Matilda to rest.

Aleen.

"You must relinquish your hold on it all," Bregdon said, as though he could sense where her thoughts had turned.

"My daughter?" she said.

"She is with your husband."

Matilda shook her head. "My husband is not—"

"He has returned," Bregdon said.

"But I did not see him return," Matilda said. She would give almost anything to see him again. Her life? Perhaps.

"He is a changed man," Bregdon said. He sucked in a hiss of a breath. "That much time with the trolls would change anyone."

"The trolls?" Matilda said. She sat up straighter. "All this time he was with the trolls?"

"Plotting his escape," Bregdon said.

"And you did not tell me?"

Bregdon spread out his hands. "I have only just now learned it."

Matilda marveled. "I must speak with him."

Bregdon's face shifted on a wave of concern. "I am afraid that is not permitted for the dead who live again. At least not your kind."

"My kind?"

"The Graces."

Matilda was silent for a moment. It was all much too mysterious to understand. He was asking too much of her. "What if I do not want to be a Grace?" she said. Whatever that meant.

"The choice has already been made. If you refuse it, you die." He did not deliver the words like a threat but as a factual statement. He gestured to a corner of the crypt, where a small glimmer of golden light met her eye. There was a man in the corner, with blue skin and a beard.

No, not a man.

"You used a djinn." She did not mean the words to sound accusatory, but playing with djinn magic was dangerous.

"The djinn and the cauldron." Matilda's eyes caught on the cauldron—her cauldron, the one she had made. It glowed for a moment, then faded and disappeared. "It was the only way I could rescue you from the grasp of the Grim Reaper," Bregdon said.

"What happened?" All she could remember was the burning.

"A fever of the most dangerous kind," Bregdon said. "The Grim Reaper overstepped his bounds."

Matilda did not ask about the Grim Reaper; she thought she would rather not know. But she did need to know about Graces, since she had become one—or would become one if she did not want to die.

What was the alternative to death? Everlasting life? And was that really so desirable?

"What is a Grace?" Matilda said.

"You are a watcher of the realm, a protector of the seven kingdoms," Bregdon said.

"I do not know what that means."

Bregdon smiled at her. "You have the full measure of magical powers," he said. "But to be used for the good of the realm, rather than for yourself."

She had never used her magic for herself, if one did not count her daily Tidy spells. She preferred order and cleanliness in her house, and Aleen had been so chaotic. Matilda's throat throbbed.

Bregdon continued. "You have the ability to sway the hearts and minds of people, to suggest their decisions, to play the part of Fate, so long as you are not too heavy-handed."

Matilda's mind began to spin.

"It was this or death," Bregdon said. "And now you are the first of a circle of three. You will lead them."

"Where are the others?" Matilda said.

"You must be patient, my dear." Bregdon rose to his feet, the movement slow and laborious, as though his old bones ached. Matilda wondered if it were possible to know how old he really was. He did not look ancient, but she knew he must be. "You must wait on the others. I will help you find them."

"How long?"

Bregdon studied her face for a moment and then shook his head. "It is difficult to say."

"So I will live on my own."

"In a cottage, in a new land."

"What land?"

"Lincastle."

"The land of miniature castles?" Matilda could not help the scorn that climbed her voice like it was a spiral staircase. She had heard stories of Lincastle and the people who gave everything in their lives to put on the perfect show. It was the land that had been founded before all the rest, the oldest in the realm, but its people were too weak, and their wills too bent, to rule the land. That is where Fairendale had won the right to rule.

It was all in the histories. She had never been to Lincastle, though.

Bregdon gestured toward the djinn. "Until I need you again, Kadesh." The words sounded painful, and Matilda noticed that a look of profound agony twisted the prophet's face. She did not understand it.

The djinn nodded and disappeared in a cloud of blue.

Bregdon turned to Matilda, offering a hand. "Come," he said, and as soon as she placed her hand in his, her body felt as though it were tearing apart. But the feeling only lasted a moment; they arrived in Lincastle in the blink of an eye.

She lived in a cottage deep inside the Wishing Woods of Lincastle. Bregdon showed her the Great Tree of Helomoth, which lived in the Whispering Woods of Rosehaven, and told her that the health of the tree indicated the health of the realm; she would be required to check on it, along with all the lands, every morning and evening. He walked her through the rituals of Graces. He taught her how to step in and out of the happenings around the realm, without attracting notice. He said she could only intervene once every fortnight, so it was important to choose intervention wisely.

It was only practice for now. Her true call would not

arrive until the other two Graces joined her.

She did not know she would be waiting so long. She did not know that the magical spinning wheel would be unearthed or that the cauldron would be stolen from its dragon guard and hauled to the farthest reaches of the land in the hands of another prophet by the name of Latimer, only to be confiscated by the giants of Guardia.

Nor did she know that the throne of Fairendale would take a sinister turn, her light magic unraveling with her death and the cheating of it. This was always a risk; magic is an unpredictable force. It feels no loyalty whatsoever to its creator. Sometimes, upon the death of its creator, magic dissipates, never to be seen again. Sometimes, however, it takes on a life of its own—becomes a curse rather than a piece of light. Matilda had considered this, upon the creation of the three magical items; she had simply hoped for better.

All this she would learn in the coming years as Matilda, the person she had been, became Good Cheer, the person—or tangible spirit, rather; it is difficult to categorize exactly what she is—she would be from here on out.

For now, she simply knew that she must wait. And wait she did.

Oaths

Good Cheer, who was, once upon a time, called Matilda, lies in bed and thinks about how advantageous it would be for the Graces to have the gift of a Prophetess's Sight.

There is a certain confidence that comes from knowing that the future is stable, that all will work out as it should. And Good Cheer has never been able to know this—beyond every doubt—about her interventions as Fate. She would like to know. Already she and her sisters feel so much pressure: they are only permitted to intervene as Fate once in a number of days (fourteen, to be exact), so they must pace their interventions, leave minor things to the people. She never knows if they have made the right decision. She feels these sorts of doubts every time her intervention is forbidden for a fortnight.

What if something more significant happens?

The Grim Reaper had almost taken the woman. Had she hesitated for too long? He would have gained some power—she knows this, though she does not know for certain why he would have gained power or what kind he would have gained.

The Graces did not have to intervene, however; the old woman in the woods had done it for them.

Who is this old woman? Why are there so many questions when they—the Graces—are the watchers of the realm, the protectors of the seven kingdoms?

Why are they not permitted to see what might be coming? Would it not help save the realm? Would it not better solidify their role as instruments of Fate?

She believes it would. And the belief burns in her chest.

If she could see the Old Man, she would complain loud and long about this injustice.

Good Cheer turns over in her bed. It has been years—decades—since she has seen the Old Man. How many more lives has he lived? Did he live his last one? Is he now forever gone?

In due time, Good Cheer falls asleep, her mind still focused on Sight and gifts, and it is no surprise that her dreams are filled with Visions full of great and terrible things. But the problem with being a Grace who is not also a Prophetess is that her mind cannot decipher whether these Visions are truly Visions or simply dreams.

So Good Cheer sleeps on, her blanket tangling around her limbs.

King Rezedron is lying in a large cave inside the dragon land of Eyre, as he has been doing for many moons now. He has been unable to heave his cumbersome body to its feet. It has been nearly a year since he has flown, since he has felt the sweet breath of wind against his face.

It is all because of a dark curse, a curse that came upon him while he was wearing his salamander skin. The dragons of Eyre are skilled shapeshifters and can make themselves as large as dragons and as small as bees. They can even make themselves invisible.

That cursed night Rezedron had been climbing one of the bushes that line the walls around Rosehaven, trying to hear what news hailed from Fairendale. He sensed something was wrong, but, at the time, he thought it had more to do with the news than the environment. Why had he not used his wings, instead? Why had he not simply made himself invisible? These are the questions that come in hindsight.

A thorn from a bush of white roses pierced his foot, and he could feel its poison spreading through his blood, blooming in an icy fire.

It did not take long before his foot and leg began to rot.

It will not take him much longer to die.

But the voice of the man—the sorcerer—who visited him with his nephew, Zorag, haunts his restless hours. *A world without magic is not a better world. Only a darker one.*

Once the curse began its destruction, Rezedron thought that he wanted to rid the world of magic, to prevent dragons everywhere from picking up a curse so foul and agonizing. But he knows, too, that his dragons are sustained by magic—both in their ability to shape shift and their ability to find food. Magic binds animals to the forest so the circle of life continues.

Without it—what then?

Rezedron turns his face toward the closest wall of the cave. How he wishes he could simply die.

A noise at the mouth of the cave startles him. It is his daughter, a daughter Zorag knows nothing about, a daughter Rezedron did not feel compelled to introduce to Zorag. Perhaps that was a mistake; he deserved to know about his cousin of royal blood. But she will not be queen; female dragons cannot inherit a throne in the land of Eyre. And perhaps she would like to make a life elsewhere, with other dragons, without the sting of royalty and rejection following her.

It is a shame. Nischal would make a fine dragon ruler.

"Father," Nischal says. "How are you today?"

"Much the same," Rezedron says, though the pain has spread—a pulsing, fiery agony that makes him wish he could fly himself to the Violet Sea and plunge his body into its waters. He is burning from the inside out with a cold so deep it blisters.

Rezedron and Nischal have not spoken of her cousin's visit, though he knows she has heard about it. She was out hunting while Zorag was here; she would not have met him coming or going.

"We are still working on finding an antidote," Nischal says. "A counter curse." Her violet eyes shine in the darkness of the cave.

"It is a wasted effort," Rezedron says. "I am not long in this world."

"You must not talk like that." Nischal draws closer. Even with both of them in this cave, it is not crowded in the least. It is a very large cave; Rezedron always knew how to pick the best.

"Why would I want to live?" Rezedron says. "Vyrmoss has already claimed the throne."

"The dragons would not support him if you were out there, too."

"Tell me why they do not support you."

Nischal looks at the ground, her violet eyes blazing. "Because I am a female."

"It makes no matter."

"We have never had a female ruler."

"It makes no matter!" All of Rezedron's anger—about the curse, about Zorag and his complicated questions, about his daughter—spills out, drenching the words.

Nischal looks at him, and a small light of amusement sparkles in her eyes. "There you are," she says, her voice soft and low. She pauses, then says, "You could live for me."

Rezedron feels a wave of sorrow steal his breath. When he can finally speak, he says, "I would if I could. You must believe that, Daughter."

"I do," she says. She does not look at him when she says, "But there is also your nephew."

The words hang between them.

Rezedron nearly opens his mouth to say something in reply, an apology, perhaps, but Nischal says, "We could join his cause, help bring about freedom." She lifts her head into a graceful arc. "Protecting magic, instead of destroying it." Her green-blue skin shimmers. "It is a noble cause, is it not?"

"So you knew," is all Rezedron says.

A second dragon appears, darkening the entrance to the cave for a moment. "Your daughter should know she has a cousin." Another dragon creeps in behind this one. He knows their names; they have been his daughter's friends since the very beginning. Handriss and Lago.

"What is this, an inquisition?" Rezedron shapes the words carefully—a bit of teasing, a bit of solemnity.

"An intervention," Lago says.

"We overheard a few things," Handriss says. She tilts her head, on which sit three horns—two above her eyes and one on the tip of her grass-green nose.

"Do you see what I have become?" Rezedron says, his voice nearly a whisper.

The dragons say nothing, and with their silence, they speak volumes.

Rezedron formulates his next excuse. "Erell was my brother," he says. "But I know nothing of Zorag."

"You know what he came here to tell you," Handriss says. "And perhaps that is enough."

Rezedron is silent for a long while. "I cannot even

stand on my feet," he says at last.

"Give the order, and we will move for you," Lago says. "And while we move, we will search for your antidote."

Rezedron heaves a very long breath into the cave. "Give me time," he says. "To think."

"We may not have much time," Nischal says. She leans closer to him. "You grow weaker every day, you—"

"I need time," Rezedron says, and this time his words come with a puff of smoke.

Nischal backs away, as do the others.

"And in the meantime?" Handriss says.

"Inquire about an antidote," Rezedron says. "I will send for you when I have made my decision."

Handriss and Lago leave the cave, but Nischal remains for a moment. Rezedron is gentle with his words. "Go, Daughter," he says. "I would like to be alone."

And Nischal does, but Rezedron finds no rest. He tosses and turns, thinking about his nephew, thinking about the curse, thinking about magic.

Thinking, for the first time, of the possibility that there might be a future.

Her plans are coming together. Yasmin walks—paces, really—among the shadows of the forest. She feels the tension inside her, the warring of the light, or who she was, with the dark, who she is now. She is being pulled one way and another, but her creatures will help her choose the way of victory.

Which is, of course, the darkness.

Is it the darkness? The wispy voice continues its questioning. Yasmin shakes her head.

Call them, another voice says. This one is stronger, more solid.

So she does.

She calls them gently, with a murmur and a click. She says the words of the Summoning spell. She waits. They gather all around her, hundreds of them—could it be thousands? They have certainly multiplied, as she commanded them to do—and in so little time. Their magic must be strong. Some are more fearsome than others; some are uglier than others. Some look as though they were experiments gone wrong. Yasmin loves them all.

Does she love them?

Yes, of course.

But really?

"Hello, my loves," Yasmin says, if only to silence the

belligerent voices.

A massive spider, the one she called Spraiko, she remembers, moves forward and positions himself in what she might call an arachnid bow. He is the leader of her army. He is the leader of the queen's guard. The thought makes her smile. She tries to ignore the way her lips tremble at their edges.

She is not entirely certain why she has been commanded to call the creatures, but she improvises by saying, "It is time to multiply beyond these woods," and the words sound true enough. She adds more: "It is time to create monsters in every land of this realm." An unstoppable army of creatures.

Instead of gathering her monsters, instead of planning her militaristic strategy, instead of committing one way or another, she will scatter them for a time. They will increase in number. She will have at her back a massive army—the largest and most fearsome one ever seen.

The monsters hold completely still, all eyes trained on her. She feels no fear, but she also feels no pride, and this is disappointing.

Yasmin holds up a stone, one that feels hollow but one that she knows is swollen with magic; it is a calling stone, hollowed out so that she can speak into it and awaken its ancient magic. It will gather her creatures from the farthest corners of the earth when it is time to assemble her army.

She tells them as much. They continue to stare. She wonders if they know what she is saying. Should she speak in another language, and, if so, what language would that be?

But Spraiko surprises her by nodding—as well as any massive spider might manage to nod.

Yasmin nods back. They understand one another.

"I will call you when it is time," Yasmin says, for good measure.

What she does not say, what she keeps hidden in the deepest recesses of her mind, is that perhaps with their help, perhaps with a large enough army of monsters, she will be able to cut loose from the one who is holding her.

Perhaps she will be free to make her own choices.

Yasmin flicks her hand, and the monsters scatter.

The Enchantress and the Huntsman wake in their clearing. Their bodies ache.

The Huntsman is lying flat on his back, but his legs are crumpled up beneath him, as though he fell to his knees first and then fell immediately backward. The Enchantress is lying face down and, in fact, has pieces of the forest floor in her mouth when she raises her head. She spits them out. One arm is raised above her, and the other was fixed over her nose—was she covering it? She does not remember. Her legs are crossed at the ankles, as though someone has rearranged her to look like a pretty red-haired doll.

She scrambles up quickly. The Huntsman stirs beside her. Her foot had been touching his. He struggles to sit up, too. His eyes look as though something blasted cold air into them, and his hair looks the same.

"I feel…windblown," he says.

It is early evening. The Enchantress feels a thin haze over her mind. Had it not been night moments ago? The Huntsman lifts himself and seems to be wondering the same thing, since his eyes are focused on the sky.

"What happened?" the Enchantress says. Her nose is sore. She must have fallen on it. She rubs it, and a burning flares.

"I believe we might have encountered a Bonnacon," the Huntsman says.

"A what?" the Enchantress says. It sounds like something the Huntsman made up.

"It is a dangerous creature," the Huntsman says. "It

releases toxic fumes from its…" He gestures toward his hind end.

"What?" the Enchantress says. Surely this is a fictitious creature. Some boy had a little fun with that one.

"We were asleep," the Huntsman says. "Though I do not know for how long."

The Enchantress rubs her nose again. The sting is nearly unbearable. She glances at the Huntsman. His nose is red, as though it has been scorched. The Huntsman catches her looking. He rubs his own nose. "The fumes must have burned us," he says.

The Enchantress shakes her head. She feels as though she is living one ridiculous hoax after another. First the egg and now a Bonnacon— a creature that blows noxious fumes out its…

Well.

The Enchantress looks toward the cart and the mare. The cages are untouched. At least there is that. They are blurry, and she cannot count them, but she does not see how any could have disappeared, with her Protection spell cloaking them.

"What is that awful smell?" the Enchantress says.

"Residue," the Huntsman says. "From the Bonnacon."

The Enchantress presses her hand to her mouth. She feels inclined to laugh again. The Huntsman's eyes crinkle.

"It is real," he says, and she bursts out laughing. The Huntsman laughs, too, while he continues saying, "I read about them once. I have never encountered one."

"Oh," the Enchantress says. She positions her arm across her nose. "It really is bad."

"We should move on," the Huntsman says. "The smell will likely remain, and most people are not as fortunate as we have been. At least according to the stories."

The Enchantress remembers, in a flash, that the creature breached her Protection spell, which means her spell was not strong enough.

Her magic is growing weaker, because she is growing weaker.

The Huntsman strides to the cart with the blackbirds, which sits in the middle of the large clearing. "Would you like to ride?" he says. "I know you need the rest."

The Enchantress gestures to the ground. "But I have already rested." She peers up at the sky. "For at least a day."

"You need more than that," the Huntsman says.

She does not disagree. She feels exceedingly weary.

She walks toward him, toward the cart, where she might lie down for a while, let the Huntsman take the lead; he has proven he can do it. She trusts him.

When she has reached him it is with a small voice that she says, "How do you think that creature got through my defenses?" It should, in theory, be impossible. She has protected them with both a Concealment spell, where they will be invisible to all who encounter them, and a Protection spell. Magical creatures should not be able to penetrate her walls.

She remembers that her magic did not work on fairies, either. Perhaps they were behind this latest breach. Perhaps this was a result of the blinding light she and the Huntsman saw.

The Huntsman does not assuage her doubts when he says, "I do not know why." He looks troubled, as though there is much more bothering him, but he remains silent.

The Enchantress has just stepped onto the cart carrying the blackbirds—blackbirds she counts, blackbirds that only number five, not six—when the Huntsman gives a cry from behind her. She turns around and gazes at the large cream-colored oval in his hands.

It is an egg.

On the ground beside the Huntsman, half hidden by trees and tall grasses and artfully placed shadows, is a very large troll, flat on his back. It is larger even than the goblin the Huntsman battled in—which woods? The Enchantress cannot remember; she only knows it was a vicious and heart-stopping battle. One foot of this creature is about the size of the Enchantress's leg, from knee to ankle. She squints to see the troll's head. It has what looks like clouds for hair, sticking straight up. Its squinty eyes are still open, and its very large nose has the same burn tint that the Huntsman's nose has. Its skin is a greenish gray color. It must have come into contact with the fumes; it was not so lucky as they were.

The Enchantress tries to speak, but she cannot.

"The egg," the Huntsman says. "We found the egg." He looks back at her. His eyes move from her to the blackbirds, back to the egg. He says his next words slowly. "Shall we put it in a cage?"

The Enchantress shakes her head. It is about all she can do.

She wills herself to speak, and it works. Her throat is tight when she says, "One of the children is missing."

The Huntsman lifts his eyes to hers, and in them she sees the same fear that blasts through her chest: They have lost a child; will they find this child again?

And what will they do with an egg?

Across the way, on the other side of Lincastle from where the Enchantress and the Huntsman have encountered the fearsome Bonnacon, Bryce wakens. She is a majestic black dragon with scales that shimmer like the beads of an expensive bracelet or necklace worn by the people of Lincastle. She has always been proud of her violet-black scales, though she knows they will become a paler tint, almost a violet-colored gray, as age does its work in several hundred years. For now she enjoys being the most resplendent dragon in the kingdom of Daron Valley.

She is, after all, its queen. Being beautiful is expected.

Bryce has awoken for some reason. She always sleeps through the hottest part of the year; black scales are not desirable during a season with so much sun. She has never woken during the Summer Sleep. Why has she woken now?

Her eyes would not have pulled open without good reason, without an alarm from her internal system. Bryce lifts her head and looks around. No other dragons are awake. Even the watcher snores from his watching place. She will have to discipline him for that; though not many venture into the land of Daron Valley, there are still those who would like the perfect opportunity—such as a watcher sleeping—to eliminate her dragons. They say the dragons of Daron Valley are too vicious, but what they really mean is they want their skins.

Bryce looks around and pats a cream-colored egg.

She looks around again. There used to be two eggs.

Someone has stolen her egg.

Bryce releases a roar that shakes the world.

In the village of Lincastle, the people who walk the streets gaze up at the sky, and a single thought moves through them as though they are one: *It is happening.* The boy charged with ringing the storm bell does his duty, immediately and vigorously, and a clanging joins the rumble. The people of Lincastle stand for a moment and then erupt into action. They have, after all, heard stories about the storm that arose from the sea and very nearly dragged all of Lincastle underwater.

If they had taken a moment to study the heavens, if they had swallowed their fear and allowed logic to replace it, they might have noticed the blue sky with not a cloud in sight.

And perhaps they would have known that the danger of a storm from the sea is nothing compared to the danger that is coming.

Don't miss the next Fairendale adventure!

Find out what happens when an old crone meets a fierce girl who attracts beasts in Book 14: *The Girl who Befriended Red-Rose.*

An Interview with Yasmin

Transcribed by L.R. Patton
Author

L.R.: I'm sure our readers are curious to know more about you, Yasmin. You have usurped the throne of Fairendale, and for what?

Yasmin: Why are your eyes closed?

L.R.: Pardon me?

Yasmin: Why are your eyes closed? You are not looking at me.

L.R.: [Peeling open one eye and trying not to screech] Yes, well…

Yasmin: You are frightened of me, too?

L.R.: You are saddened by people's fright?

Yasmin: When it is directed at me, yes. I am not a monster.

L.R.: [clears throat] No, you are not.

Yasmin: You think me a monster?

L.R.: No, I think…this interview is not about me; it is about you.

Yasmin: I will not answer any questions unless they are asked while looking at me.

L.R.: [squaring shoulders] As you wish.

Yasmin: It is my bluish skin, is it?

L.R.: Well, it *is* unusual.

Yasmin: But no less beautiful.

L.R.: No. You are correct. It is no less beautiful.

Yasmin: Now can we move on?

L.R.: Yes. I believe I did ask you a question. Why do you want the Fairendale throne?

Yasmin: I am not entirely sure.

L.R.: You are…can you explain to us all how you do not know why you want the throne?

Yasmin: I never wanted a throne. At least I do not think I did. But something magnetic drew me toward Fairendale. It was not my own doing.

L.R.: Who…?

Yasmin: I believe I was sent by the Grim Reaper.

L.R.: You do know who the Grim Reaper is, do you not?

Yasmin: The ruler of the dead. Yes. I was dead.

L.R.: And yet here you are.

Yasmin: And yet here I am, if not entirely.

L.R.: Not entirely—what do you mean by that?

Yasmin: I am not entirely in the world of the living and not entirely in the world of the dead. I am an outcast.

L.R.: It must be a very lonely place for you to be.

Yasmin: Yes, well, what need have I of people? [Clears throat.]

L.R.: None?

Yasmin: Precisely.

L.R.: So if you do not know why you want a throne —or, rather, the Grim Reaper wants a throne—what do you plan to do with it?

Yasmin: I suppose what anyone would do with a throne: rule it. For as long as I am able.

L.R.: And will you be a good ruler?

Yasmin: Can anyone say whether or not she will be a good ruler?

L.R.: No, I suppose one cannot.

Yasmin: I feel light-headed, as though I am fading. Am I fading?

L.R.: I can see through you now. Oh, dear. There is a creature behind you. I have never seen such a ghastly sight! Wait!

Yasmin: What is happening?

L.R.: Yasmin?

Yasmin:

L.R.: I do apologize, dear reader, but I am afraid I must cut short this lovely time with you. This fearsome creature looks none too happy about Yasmin disappearing like that, and I do not want to get caught in his wrath—Oh! Oh no! Oh, stay away, creature! Shoo! Go on, now! Aaaaaghhh!

If you would like [gasp] to read more [gasp] Fairendale extras like this [gasp], be sure to visit [gasp] www.lrpatton.com/fairendale.

I hope I will see you next time! Aaaaaghhh!

How to Live Forever

By Bregdon, also known as the Old Man Prophet of White Wind

It was never my intention to live forever, you must understand that. Something happened when I faked my own death to escape from the Prophet Rip, who was once a very close friend and colleague. This story is much too long to recount here (it will be told in a future book, so your narrator assures me); I mention it only to say that I woke up from a faked death and I have never been able since to die a proper death.

Many long to live forever. It is true that life can be very, very good, and one wants to prolong it as much as one might be permitted. But I have watched so many people die—my friends, my family, my acquaintances even. It is not an easy thing to be separated from them as I am. One never thinks of this when one wishes to live forever.

I do hope that I can accomplish as much good as I possibly can in the time I have remaining me—and who knows how long that is: forever, or not quite?

Your narrator asked me to write a short piece on how one might live forever. I begrudgingly agreed, but only for the purpose of historical recording. Not many know of these Everlasting Life elixirs, items, and pools any longer, and I hope that you will not attempt to follow in the footsteps of those who once did: not one lives to tell about their quests.

Here are some foolish ways to attempt living forever:

1. Find the Elixir of Life.

This elixir is said to be hidden somewhere near the land of Eastermoor. It is produced by a stream that is said to flow straight from a strangely shaped rock, as though it wells from the ground and not from the sea. It was once rumored that those who found and drank the elixir were immediately transformed into Were creatures, as a consequence for attempting to live forever. Some say, to mollify their own consciences, that Were creatures are given the elixir upon becoming Were creatures—by whom no one ever postulated. Since no one has ever spoken with a Were creature, there is no telling which version is true. Suffice it to say: stay away from the Elixir of Life, unless becoming a Were creature is your goal.

2. Eat from the Tree of Life.

This tree, according to legend, stands somewhere in Guardia and is guarded by one of the fiercest dragons you ever saw—except that you will not see this dragon; she is invisible. Ancient stories tell of those who tried to pick the fruit of the tree, which was similar to that of a frozen apple with a bit of cream inside (though if no one has ever tasted it, how would they know?), and were immediately attacked by an invisible dragon. It is anyone's guess how the tellers of these stories knew it was a dragon.

3. The Everlasting Pool of Shual.

This pool is rumored to be somewhere between Rosehaven and Fairendale, on the road north. There are many pools along this road, home to more goblin kingdoms than one would like to know. Because of this, not many have explored the pools to see if the Everlasting Pool of Shual exists. It is understandably so; if one steps into a pool that lies on top of an underground goblin kingdom, one can assume that one's life is over as is. Is a pool that claims to grant everlasting life worth spending the rest of your life—perhaps even forever—as a goblin slave?

4. The Golden Grail.

Said to reside somewhere at the bottom of the Violet Sea, this gem-encrusted chalice is supposed to have supernatural properties that include healing, magic, wealth, and eternal youth. No one knows exactly where in the Violet Sea the Golden Grail was last seen, and the sea is large and expansive—searching it would not likely result in much of anything, except annoying mermaids (who are not nearly as accommodating and kind as you might have been led to believe in the stories you have heard in your life) and their King, Tritanius. Stories tell of many men and women who tried to find the Golden

Grail and were never seen again, whether because they discovered it and were given a new life or because the mermaids never let them return to their life above the sea.

5. The Diamond of Ozria.

This diamond is said to be somewhere in the land of White Wind, and it is partly the reason so many used to visit White Wind, though not the only. The snow in White Wind has a magical quality about it that makes it appear to be made of diamonds. The legend of this diamond has mostly faded away, so not as many people know about it anymore—but once the land had many intruders searching for its everlasting gem. In a land with perpetual snow (yes, even in the springtime) that looks like diamonds, it is a fools' errand to go searching for one in particular, though stories tell of how this one is different: it resembles a miniature glacier, with layers and edges and crests that, when examined in the full sunlight, shine a silvery blue.

Many of the stories told about these conduits of everlasting life were told by the explorer of these lands, a man named Dale Enderling, who was not always the most rational man and was historically given to flights of fancy. Some of his observations, recorded in a volume of thick journals, were disregarded after it was noted that for much of his exploration, King Enderling (as he would one day be called in Lincastle) was in dire need of spectacles, which he lost on his journey by ship.

However, those who spend their whole lives searching for these elixirs, items, and pools, still exist, though I cannot fathom what would possess someone to spend their entire life on something so questionable. Most of us (I am the exception, I suppose) only have one life. We must live it well.

How Dragons Communicate: an Exploration

By Arthur of Fairendale

Former teacher of magical studies, friend of dragons

Dragons have very intricately-run societies, but how they communicate was largely somewhat of a mystery until the journals of one who studied them (unfortunately we do not know to whom these journals belonged) was found in an excavation near the land of Ashvale.

Here are some interesting facts we learned from these journals about the ways dragons communicate.

Dragons speak telepathically with one another.

Dragons of different regions and kingdoms have variations in their languages. For example, the dragons in the north do not have nearly as extensive a vocabulary as the ones in Fairendale, but this is likely because they were not in touch with humans as frequently as the dragons of Morad, and they had no access to books. The dragons of Morad, on the other hand, were told all sorts of stories by none other than Prince Wendell, back before he was banished from the kingdom.

In spite of these variations, the dragons seem to share

a universal language. Perhaps it is part of their magic: they speak in their own language and it is magically translated into the language of another dragon, telepathically (meaning inside their minds).

It must be noted that this telepathic communication is quite unnerving if you are a human in the presence of more than one dragon; they will communicate with one another and you will be unable to hear it. Some fortunate individuals are gifted with hearing the telepathic communication of dragons—a gift reserved for most dragon riders and any other individuals dragons decide to bequeath with the universal language (one cannot study this language; it is a gift in all circumstances. This, too, is a mysterious thing.). If you do not have the gift of telepathic communication, you will have to study the faces and fire of dragons (a frightful thing, to be sure) to attempt an understanding of what they may not want you to hear.

Dragons speak out loud to humans.

They do this for a number of purposes: to be heard, of course, but also to appear more intimidating. If one has ever heard the speech of a dragon, one will know precisely why I call it intimidating. They speak with a loud rumble that sounds like a cross between a roar springing up from the earth, a growl from the heavens, and a beastly shout, if you can imagine that. It is a frightful thing, and sometimes they do it simply to make a human cower.

Dragons speak with physical marks.

They do not have to discuss boundary lines; they merely leave their marks. These marks vary from dragon species to dragon species, but if one is well versed in the ways of dragons, one can always recognize where a dragon community begins and ends. The dragons of Morad, for example, mark their trees with a straight line etched out by a claw and a burned spot on the bark above it, which looks a bit like a candle with a flame. It is highly artistic—as any mark of a dragon will be.

Dragons speak in their posture and body language.

This is an important concept to know and understand: a dragon can be read as much by his posture as his words. Sometimes, in fact, what he is saying verbally and what he is saying nonverbally, with his body, can be two very different things. One should always believe what the dragon is saying with his body. So here are some clues to consider.

A stiff, rigid body posture usually indicates that the dragon is annoyed or growing angry (at which point you should watch out for his fire, for it is coming).

A relaxed body posture with a dipped head indicates a dragon is comfortable in your presence.

If a dragon twitches every now and then (you can see this on the skin if you observe well enough), it means that he is hesitant to trust you and must give it a bit more time and space before he can decide one way or another. Do not push your luck.

Dragons also allow their eyes to speak for them. This is a bit more mysterious and open to interpretation, as one must know a particular dragon in order to read the eyes (though some humans, of course, are gifted with this ability regardless of whether a dragon is a friend or a stranger). This point is somewhat complicated by the fact that it is an unsettling thing to stare into a dragon's eyes, trying to decode what a dragon is feeling. Dragon eyes are not always easy to observe—but if you find yourself courageous enough to do it, you can read emotions there.

For example, let us imagine a dragon with yellow eyes. Here are some emotions you might be able to read in a dragon's yellow eyes.

Pale yellow: wary or shy (try to get on their good side)

Bright yellow: interested or happy (keep doing what you are doing)

Glowing yellow: very angry (you should run)

These are only a few of the shades that can be detected and decoded in the eyes of a dragon.

Dragons use their tails to communicate as well—almost as a cat might. If their tails twitch playfully (generally this is only seen in the very young), it indicates a playful demeanor. If they sweep the ground with their tail in an aggressive flicking fashion, it likely means they are feeling annoyed and on their way to anger. If they thump the ground with their tail, they might be thinking. If they swing their tail at you, well, I am sure you can deduce what this means.

Dragons speak with their fire.

Fire means one thing: infuriation, which translates in human terms to "imminent death." If you hear the fire rumbling in the belly of a dragon, run as fast as you can and hope it is fast enough.

It must be said that these tips and interpretations are recorded and observed by humans, which is to say they are subject to human error and fallibility. One must always use one's powers of observation in the presence of dragons. It is the only thing worth relying on in the end.

How to Enrage a Dragon—As If You Would Want To

By L.R. Patton
Author

Of course there are many, many ways to enrage a dragon, because dragons are temperamental creatures. But here are three of the most dangerous ways:

1. Trespassing

It is probably safer to stay away from lands known to harbor dragons. If you cannot avoid them, tread carefully. That is to say: silently. Do not make a sound. If you do, beware.

2. Insult them

If you happen to come into contact with a dragon, it is wiser to say nothing than to say something that risks offending that dragon. And, as we have already established, dragons are temperamental creatures; one never knows what words will offend them. Better to use as few as possible—or none at all.

3. Steal an egg

An egg is a highly valuable commodity to a dragon— not only because inside them is a baby dragon growing toward hatching but also because they are not so easily replaced (neither, of course, is any child or human or creature; life is life). Most of the dragons in our story only lay one egg every one hundred or so years. This makes them remarkably precious—and a thief remarkably dead.

Stay away from the eggs.

In fact, it is wise to simply stay away from dragons.

You have been warned.

The Royal Family of Fairendale

King Willis: The current king of Fairendale. Son of King Sebastien. Has a deep love for sweet rolls.

Queen Clarion: The current queen of Fairendale. Is underestimated by her husband and most of the kingdom, but she will prove just how powerful she is in due time.

Prince Virgil: Son of King Willis and Queen Clarion, best friend of Theo. Prefers rye bread with melted butter to sweet rolls, depending on the day. Currently exists as a blackbird, transformed by the sorceress Cora.

King Sebastien: Deceased king of Fairendale, exception to the line of boys who tried to steal thrones and were, upon failing at their quest, forever banished. Was killed by a blackbird. Now lives, as much as the dead can live, inside a magic mirror.

The Former Royal Family of Fairendale

The Good King Brendon: Former king of Fairendale responsible for the alliance between the people of Fairendale and the dragons of Morad, lost the throne when it was stolen by King Sebastien. Killed in the Great Battle.

Queen Marion: Wife of the Good King Brendon, died mysteriously when her daughter was very young. Now lives in Lincastle and is "affectionately" called the Evil Queen.

Princess Maren: Daughter of the Good King Brendon and Queen Marion. She has been missing since the Great Battle.

The Villagers of Fairendale

Arthur: Village furniture maker and magic instructor to girls who possess the gift of magic in the village of Fairendale. Is a bit reckless but always manages to come out all right on the other side—though one is not always assured it will be so.

Maude: Arthur's wife. Bakes spectacular pumpkin spice sugar cookies. Prefers caution to reckless abandon.

Hazel: Daughter of Arthur and Maude, twin of Theo. Cares for the village sheep and can even, amazingly, understand them. 12 years old.

Theo: Son of Arthur and Maude, twin of Hazel. Finishes his chores early so he can sit in on magic lessons. 12 years old. (Also known as the Huntsman, after a complicated Transformation spell turned him five years older and much ruddier than before.)

Mercy: Red-haired daughter of Cora, best friend of Hazel. Prefers spectacular acts of magic to "boring" ones.

Cora: Mother of Mercy, widow, sorceress, shape shifter with the form of a blackbird. A woman who moves. Unofficial leader of the village people in Fairendale who falls in and out of favor with them. Has become a dragon rider and somehow misplaced most of her magical powers.

Garron: The town gardener. Talks to plants as though they can hear him.

Bertie: The town baker. Enjoys showing off his air-kneading skills for the children—or used to. There is no longer much wheat with which to bake anymore.

Staff of Fairendale Castle

Garth: Page for King Willis, the oldest of twelve children. No longer calls King Willis "Your Wideness" when he is feeling particularly prickly, because he knows how dishonoring it is to call names.

Cook (Mira): One of the few shape shifters in the land. Shape shifts into a bear. Is highly annoyed by her assistant, Calvin—but not really.

Calvin: An orphan who began working as Cook's assistant after his parents died in a Fire Mountain eruption in Ashvale. He is the only one allowed through the magical door to the dungeons beneath the dungeons and so is tasked with feeding the prisoners and keeping them alive.

Sir Greyson: Captain of the king's guard. Receives medicine, which keeps his mother alive, for his service to the king. Carries a magical sword that cannot be lifted by any but him—and is the only sword that can kill a shape shifter.

Sir Merrick: Second in command to Sir Greyson. Has a blind daughter named Agnes. Disappeared in dragon fire when crossing the lands of Morad. Presumed dead.

Gus, Timmy, Florence: Three blind, talking mice. Not technically staff of the castle, but they roam about it unseen, gathering information. It is suggested they were once people, transformed by a spell.

Important Prophets

Aleen: Prophetess from the kingdom of White Wind who lived one hundred forty-three years. Wears ebony skin and what appears to be snakes for hair (though it is not). Sacrificed her life to change the fate of the Fairendale children in Book 6.

Yerin: Prophet who is one hundred forty-two years old, from the wild woodland between Lincastle and Eastermoor. Has white hair that makes the dark of the dungeons where he is imprisoned a bit less dark.

Folen: Former prophet of Lincastle, father of Iddo. Trapped in a looking glass created by Queen Marion. It was left on the grounds of Fairendale, just before the Great Battle.

Iddo: Prophet of Lincastle, son of Folen. Trained King Sebastien in both dark and light magic, though he is more scientist than sorcerer. Created a machine that can bring the dead to life again. It has only worked once.

Bregdon: Prophet of White Wind. Most powerful prophet in the land, known as the Old Man. Wrote and enchanted the Old Man's Great Book. Brought Queen Marion and the three Graces back to life. Lives life after life after life in a seemingly everlasting way.

Dragons of Morad

Zorag: King of the dragons of Morad. Wears green scales with an ivory belly. Lost his parents in the Great Battle, when King Sebastien stole the throne from the

Good King Brendon. Would like nothing more than peace.

Blindell: Zorag's cousin, raised as the dragon king's son. Wears black scales and spikes all down his back. Lost his parents in the Great Battle, when King Sebastien stole the throne from the Good King Brendon. Would like nothing more than revenge.

Larus: One of the elder dragons of Morad, male. Counselor to Zorag. Wears blue-green scales that shimmer like water. Has a green horn on the top of his snout.

Malera: One of the elder dragons of Morad, female. Counselor to Zorag. Wears bright red scales and an ivory belly.

Alvah: One of the elder dragons of Morad, female. Counselor to Zorag. Ancient dragon who has been alive since before Zorag's father was born. Wears orange scales that used to be red but have faded in time.

Oned: One of the elder dragons of Morad, male. Counselor to Zorag. So ancient he is gray, colorless, with scales peeled off in places.

Kohar: Ancient food gatherer for the dragons of Morad, male. Wears pale yellow scales.

Other Important Dragons

Rezedron: King of the dragons of Eyre, uncle of Zorag. Dying of wounds sustained from a poisonous rose in Rosehaven, believed to be dark magic.

Nischal: Rezedron's daughter. Unlikely to become queen of the dragons of Eyre, because of a law that forbids a female to inherit the throne.

Residents of the Violet Sea

Arya: Twelfth daughter of King Tritanius, who rules the Violet Sea. Adventurous, impulsive, often considered rebellious by her father. Saves the Huntsman from death by fairy magic. Loves a mortal.

Other Important Characters

The Graces: Formerly mortal women who died and were brought back to eternal life by the Old Man. Now known as Splendor, Good Cheer, and Mirth, or, collectively, the Graces. Maintain the balance of good and evil in the realm. Cannot predict the future; can only influence it.

The Grim Reaper: Master of the dead. Leads an army of Black-Eyed Beings. Longs to be seen as something more than a passing shadow.

Yasmin: Frankenstein-like creature brought back to life by the scientific tools of Iddo. Formerly known as Gladys, mother of Sebastien (future king of Fairendale, but not in her lifetime).

The lost 12-year-old children of Fairendale

Ursula

Chester

Charles

Thumbelina (known as Lina among the children)

Minnie

Jasper: Transported to the land of White Wind by Hazel's Vanishing spell. Becomes a wolf who befriends a girl in a red cloak. Runs very fast.

Frederick

Ruby: Transported to the land of Rosehaven by Hazel's Vanishing spell. Becomes an old woman who meets Rapunzel, befriends her, and supplies her with chamomile. She is a masterful gardener.

Martin

Oscar: Transported to the land of Lincastle by Hazel's Vanishing spell. Remains exactly the same, even down to the holes in his boots. Loves to read, steals food by pretending to be a bird, and befriends a princess (he would never admit it is, more precisely, a crush).

Homer: Transported to the land of Rosehaven by Hazel's Vanishing spell. Becomes a dwarf who can spin straw into gold, otherwise known as Rumpelstiltskin.

Anna: Transported to the land of Eastermoor by Hazel's Vanishing spell. Becomes an old, bent woman who resides in the Were Woods. Is awkward with magic, which causes some unexpected problems.

Aurora

Rose

Edgar

Harriet (known as Hattie among the children)

Isabel (known as Izzy among the children)

Ralph

Dorothy

Julian

Tom Thumb

Philip: Transported to the forest outside Lincastle by Hazel's Vanishing spell. Becomes the leader of the Merry Men, otherwise known as Robin Hood. Can shoot an arrow straight to the target, even if the arrow is crooked.

Other lost children of Fairendale

August: One of the lost boys of Fairendale, escaped with Theo. Known as the leader of the lost boys. Resides in a rundown shelter in Lincastle. 11 years old.

Leopold: One of the lost boys of Fairendale, escaped with Theo. Resides with August and the other lost boys. 11 years old.

Fineas: One of the lost boys of Fairendale, escaped with Theo. Formerly resided with August and the other lost boys, but was captured by the fairies of Never Land. 11 years old.

Norman: One of the lost boys of Fairendale, escaped with Theo. Resides with August and the other lost boys. 10 years old.

Henry: One of the lost boys of Fairendale, escaped with Theo. Resides with August and the other lost boys. 10 years old.

Ernest: One of the lost boys of Fairendale, escaped with Theo. Resides with August and the other lost boys. 10 years old.

Agnes: Daughter of Sir Merrick, trapped in the dungeons beneath the dungeons of Fairendale castle. Blind, but quite good at hearing and sensing what others cannot.

About the Author

L.R. has never ruled a throne in the literal sense, but metaphorically speaking, she co-rules the throne of her home-kingdom, sharing cooking duties, child-raising duties, nighttime routine duties, and many other duties with her partner, King Ben. And while she does not create beastly monsters with a magical pen, she does awaken grumpy beast-like creatures every morning and listens to them growl about breakfast and signs their folders and agendas with a pen that can be considered magical for the simple fact of its existence—it has not yet disappeared.

When she is not ruling her throne (she never stole one, mind you) with patience (mostly), justice (ideally), and love (always, she hopes); corralling beastly boys out the door; and creating magic with her pen, L.R. likes to sit in her throne-like dust-blue wing chair and read about the adventures of others.

L.R. shares her castle in San Antonio, Texas, with King Ben and their six young princes, who try, multiple times a day, to steal an imaginary throne from one another—about once every 2.5 minutes, to be exact.

www.lrpatton.com

A Note From L.R.

Dear Reader,

Life sometimes unfolds circumstances that feel too large for us, that make us feel decidedly small, that diminish and discourage us. The best way to pull through those kinds of circumstances is to remember who you are: strong, kind, courageous, beloved child. You are worth more than diamonds and thrones and the richest of kingdoms. I hope you always remember that even at your worst—when you usurp thrones or create beastly creatures (or become one yourself) or execute plans that do not appear to value and honor humanity as well as we all should—you are still loved. There is nowhere you can go, nothing you can do, that will eliminate this ridiculous, extravagant love that enfolds you.

Now how will you gift your love to others?

I pour my love into my stories. I believe in their power to inspire, inform, multiply love, and effect real change in the lives of readers. And I write every book with this (noble, I hope) purpose in mind.

Though my writing is done alone, my world-changing is not. I need readers like you to help get my books into the hands of those who don't yet know the hope and inspiration that can be found in them. So here are some ways you can help:

1. Leave a review on Amazon.

Reviews help other readers find my books. The more readers who find my book, the better I am able to accomplish what I've listed above.

2. Tell your friends about this book.

Word of mouth is one of the most powerful tools we have for sharing the things we love—and it is, consequently, one of the most powerful tools I have for sharing my work with new readers. Your word of mouth, spread to others.

I appreciate anything you do to help my books get into the hands of readers so that love can expand and surround and make its everlasting mark.

In love,

L.R.

Acknowledgements

Yasmin's story is not about a fairy tale character, exactly, but she does seem to favor a literary character, Frankenstein's monster, who was, like her, raised from nothing and brought to life with science. And so perhaps the first people I should thank on this list are authors of classic books (like Mary Shelley, who wrote *Frankenstein*), which provide such rich and fertile soil for the imagination, and the English teacher I remember encouraging me the most persistently to read them: Mrs. Jimerson. Thank you for showing me the beauty in these old works.

Ben—Thank you, as always, for your love and support and for questioning iffy parts in the manuscript. You will be thanked in every book, and maybe eventually I will run out of things to say and will be left with only this: I love you.

My sons—Every word out of your mouth, every silly (or not so silly) action, every day lived with you is a source of joy and inspiration. Thank you for asking me to write stories, for collaborating with me on stories, for showing me just how wonder-full a world can be.

Mom—For buying the Fairendale books and stocking them in your library. I think you're my biggest fan.

My launch team—For your continuous encouragement to keep going.

Thank you all for being who you are.

Enjoy more stories from the magical Fairendale series:

LRPatton.com/Fairendale

Starter Library

A singular obsession. A safe hiding space. A never-ending search.

The king's guard has been searching all the lands of the realm for the missing Fairendale children. But, alas, Captain Sir Greyson has returned, after many days, to report to King Willis that no children have been found. The king, quite angry at this disappointing news, orders another search, this one closer to home—right inside the dangerous Weeping Woods.

*Continue your journey into the world of Fairendale with Book 2: The King's Pursuit, a short story prequel, "The Good King's Fall" and some important bonus material, **free for a limited time.***

To get your FREE bonus materials, visit *
LRPatton.com/goodking

*Must be 13 or older to be eligible